IN THE BEGINNING

The EARLY DAYS of RELIGIOUS BELIEFS

JAIME REYES

IN THE BEGINNING

The Early Days of Religious Beliefs

JAIME REYES

Also by Jaime Reyes

En el Principio (Spanish Version)
Short Stories:
"The Shining City by the Sea"
"Lazarus Effect"

Memoirs:
First Night
Guest Columnist:
We Complain (English)
Nos Quejamos (Spanish)

Blogs:
Opciones Para el Futuro de Puerto Rico (Spanish)
Options for the Future of Puerto Rico (English)
Legalization of Marijuana

For my grandchildren and Great-Grandchildren.
Not necessarily in order of preference.

Anthony Sr & Jr	Emily
Lesley	Jasmine
Edward	Julian
Natasha	Nina
Jeramiah	Ameenah
Jaaziah	Ronin Jaime
Leah	Idris
Ivy	Leonardo

In the beginning, man created God.
—Jethro Tull

If God did not exist, it would be necessary to invent him.
—Voltaire

Which is it, is man one of God's blunders or is God one of man's?
—Friedrich Nietzsche

It is said that man may not be the dream of the Gods,
but rather that the Gods are the dreams of men.
—Carl Sagan

What gods are there, what gods have there ever been,
that were not from man's imagination.
—Joseph Campbell

TABLE *of* CONTENTS

INTRODUCTION 1

CHAPTER 1.   EPIPHANY 3
CHAPTER 2.   GROWING BELIEF AND POWER....................6
CHAPTER 3.   OG'S FAMILY PROSPERS 12
CHAPTER 4.   THE COMING OF WAR...................................14
CHAPTER 5.   CHIEF ATO 16
CHAPTER 6.   STRANGERS...18
CHAPTER 7.   THE BIG CAT..22
CHAPTER 8.   FEMALE WARRIORS...23
CHAPTER 9.   OG PONDERS DEATH 24
CHAPTER 10.   ATU AND KOR 26
CHAPTER 11.   SEEDS OF CHANGE FOR WOMEN 28
CHAPTER 12.   REVENGE..30
CHAPTER 13.   REGRETS...33
CHAPTER 14.   MINA 35
CHAPTER 15.   THE END OF OG 46

CHAPTER 16.   STALKING THE STRANGERS 49
CHAPTER 17.   PREPARING FOR THE STRANGERS 55
CHAPTER 18.   DISCOVERING PELU AND HIS TRIBE 58
CHAPTER 19.   HEADING INTO THE STORM..................... 62
CHAPTER 20.   TONG'S TRIBE 64
CHAPTER 21.   PELU'S VILLAGE 67
CHAPTER 22.   AMBASSADOR EXCHANGE 73
CHAPTER 23.   STRANGERS IN FOREIGN LANDS 76
CHAPTER 24.   NITO'S RETURN 81
CHAPTER 25.   SIGNS OF DANGER..................................... 84
CHAPTER 26.   SAVING THE FAMILY.................................. 86
CHAPTER 27.   THE MARCH TO WAR................................. 90
CHAPTER 28.   VILLAGE ASSAULT 92
CHAPTER 29.   SURVIVORS 96
CHAPTER 30.   MINA'S REVENGE 98
CHAPTER 31.   FAMILY REUNION.......................................102
CHAPTER 32.   ASSIMILATION 104
CHAPTER 33.   SPREADING THE WORD OF OG.............106

EPILOGUE 111
HISTORICAL NOTES 112
ABOUT THE AUTHOR..118
SOURCES 119
FYI...121
CONTACT THE AUTHOR 122

INTRODUCTION

Religious assemblies, from Christianity to Judaism, Islam, Hinduism, and so forth, and the various factions of each, are among the most powerful organizations ever created. Unlike the Supreme Being they purport to speak for, they have not always existed. As an anonymous writer once said, they are "the figments of someone else's imagination." All religious beliefs had a beginning. Someone, sometime, somewhere, came up with the idea. It may have been an epiphany, an invention formed out of necessity, or just a harebrained idea. Regardless of the source of inspiration, one person or a small group of like-minded individuals produced a germ of an idea that blossomed into a power designed primarily for some form of profit and in order to manipulate or control others. It is conceivable that some religious innovators initially had more altruistic intentions, but in time, the innovation evolved into disguised business enterprises. Others corrupted the original intent and warped the idea to instill a fear that would serve to maintain control over the masses via way of threats of punishment or penance while living, torture or human sacrifice, and finally, eternal damnation.

Early protohumans like Neanderthals and Cro-Magnon buried their dead and cared for their sick and injured. In order to understand the unexplainable or to establish answers to questions such as, "Where does the sun come from and where does it go? What brings rain?" They turned to mysticism or imagined invisible beings. It is safe to assume that they experienced some form of primitive spiritual awareness. It is also not hard to believe that someone had to become the first priest, shaman, spirit guide, or witch doctor to realize the benefit of organizing and exploiting such primitive notions. This is the story of such a person.

Not considered is divine inspiration; otherwise, the era of polytheism could then be excluded from history.

The only questionable assumption is the when. It could have been one hundred thousand years ago, half of that, or perhaps double that. This is a fictionalized version of the earliest use of religious persuasion and the first person to take advantage of the power that comes with the assumption of priesthood.

Just as da Vinci was ahead of his time in the Middle Ages, Og was an exceptionally intelligent cave dweller.

The premise of this fictional tale is that one such exceptional early man out of necessity found a way to convince his tribal troupe that he had the answers to their fears and apprehensions. An idea or a lie oft repeated soon becomes accepted fact, and once cemented into the psyche, it becomes near impossible to dislodge that implanted conviction.

As Voltaire is reported to have said, "The first clergyman was the first rascal who met the first fool."

CHAPTER 1
EPIPHANY

Circa 40,000 BC

Og sat in his cave, sheltered from the vicious deluge. He was ancient for people of that era and was understandably tired. He knew that if he did not hunt with the tribe, he would not eat. He was in relatively good health but was neither fast nor agile anymore, and he did not want to be stomped by a mastodon, mauled by a giant bear, or eaten by a long tooth.

There must be a better way to survive, he thought, while the thunderous storm grew in intensity and fury.

He saw some of the younger tribal members trembling in their caves or huddled in leaky huts. They had experienced storms before but not as brutal as this one. Og had lived longer than any of them and realized that this storm would pass, as had all the others. He figured that although the huts may be blown away, no storm had ever destroyed a cave. *Hmm. They are afraid, and I am not*, he thought. *How can I use this to my advantage? Yes, I know.*

He worked up his courage and went to the largest cave, where the chief cowered with his mate, children, and higher-ranking tribal members. "Chief Olo," Og said, "you know that I have been around for a long time and I have seen this before. The spirits are angry, and we must appease them!"

"How?" asked the chief.

"When I was younger, a storm like this came upon the tribe, and my father prayed to the spirit, lit fires all night, danced for it and sacrificed a village dog. This pleased the storm bringer, and there was peace again. I remember all he did, and I can do the same, but it is a difficult task.

I will be up most of the night and will not be able to join the morning hunting party. For a small share of tomorrow's hunt, I will be glad to perform the ritual, appease the angry spirit and end this problem."

The young chief had no solution of his own. He and his tribe were terrified. He had no choice but to believe the older man and agreed. Og also suggested to Olo that it would be best if villagers who were in huts moved into caves for now. The storm would not stop for some time, and Og warned that the flimsy shelters could be damaged or destroyed, along with those inside. The chief saw the wisdom of the suggestion and directed the cave-dwelling members to share and shelter those less fortunate for the night.

Og now had to provide a convincing display, whether or not he personally believed in what he intended to do. He looked in his cave for rattles, bones, or any kind of noisemaker. He quickly painted his face as if going to war, and he trapped one of the curs that frequented the village searching for scraps.

Og was now ready to try to impress the frightened tribal families. He had no real memory of what he claimed his father did, but neither did the tribe. Whatever he did would be new to them and to himself.

The would-be priest tied the doomed dog to a stake in the ground and began to prance around rattling his noisemakers, throwing bones in the air, and making up sounds and words as he continued. He gave the storm spirit a name, Ura, and yelled it often and as loud as he could.

The tribe looked on from their shelters and caves, bewildered but with growing interest. Younger children were frightened not only of the storm but of the crazy old man's antics and strange noises. The mothers held the younglings tight and tried to console them. They were afraid too but were hopeful that Og would save them from the torrential rains, lightning, and howling winds.

Og's activities tired him quickly, but he had to keep going to make a convincing display. In order to take a brief rest between dances and incantations, he fell to his knees and bowed reverently with his arms out as flashes of lightning produced an eerie backdrop of sudden spotlight for his wild gyrations. Sometimes he put his hands together in supplication as he stared at the sky and spoke to unseen, nonexistent beings. He noted the flashes of lightning and the interval between the flash and the sound of thunder. He did not know how to count but understood the concepts of time and distance. He knew that the shorter intervals between the thunder and flash of lightning meant that the spears of light were getting closer and he must take cover. Og had been alive longer than any of his people, and he had had more time to learn and understand the ways of nature. He was also quite intelligent for people of his era.

An idea came to his mind. If it worked, the display would prove his uncanny powers. He asked the chief for his longest spear—not one of the old ones tipped with sharp bone but one of the new ones made with the stone-like shards the tribe had found while exploring new caves. He recalled a previous storm when a fire bolt struck a hunter dead while carrying a metal-tipped spear.

The lightning strikes were getting closer as the storm continued to move in the village's direction. He knew he had to hurry. Out in the open, he was a target for a direct hit. He planted the chief's long spear in the middle of the cleared area around the center of the village, tied the dog securely to the spear, and moved to safety away from the open field. A short time later, as he expected, the long metal-tipped spear attracted the lightning. The fire bolt illuminated the whole of the village, and the sacrificial dog disappeared in the explosive flash. Again, Og noted the time difference between the flashes and the sound, and he came out to the village clearing when he knew he would be safe.

"Ura is pleased with the offering!" he yelled at the chief. "The storm will pass soon, and you can sleep in peace. I will continue through the night and beg the mighty storm spirit to have pity on us and to ask his brother Ka, the hunter spirit, to favor us tomorrow with a good hunt."

C H A P T E R 2
GROWING BELIEF AND POWER

The storm abated during the night as Og had hoped for, and he gleefully accepted the accompanying accolades in the morning. He also exhorted the hunters as they marched off for the day's hunt. Og was confident that the mention of the hunter spirit would give them greater confidence. The newly self-proclaimed priest knew that encouraging words did not change anything but that often they affected and energized people to maximum effort.

To Og's unexpressed surprise, the hunt was very successful. He claimed credit but also reverently thanked Ka. The clan would eat well for days. As promised, Og received a substantial share not only in bounty but also in honor and respect.

While Og planned his future as representative of the spirits and their priest, Chief Olo pondered the danger to his position as leader of the tribe. He knew that Og, by virtue of his age and experience, had some standing in the tribe. Now that he displayed some sort of power over the elements, the tribe would surely hold him in awe. The chief was afraid, especially after seeing the spear of light from the heavens obliterate the sacrificial dog. *What else can he do?* wondered Olo. *Can he make me disappear too?* Chief Olo would find it very difficult to get peaceful rest this night—and maybe others.

During the next few days after the big storm, Og experienced a definite change in the way the people reacted to him. He noticed a greater respect and, in some, a sense of wonderment directed at him by most villagers. There was one notable exception. Chief Olo kept his distance, and sometimes when Og approached the chief while he met with the elders, Olo would stop talking and make up an excuse to leave. Og was too intelligent to be puzzled by the chief's reaction. Speaker of the gods or not, Og sensed danger if the chief acted on his fears of losing control or getting displaced by an old man who had nothing but claims and incantations.

Og realized that the chief had real power in the form of young, obedient allies and relatives who would defend him in any confrontation. Olo also had weapons and youthful muscles to wield them with skill. Og only had superior wits, but that would not protect him against a deftly thrown spear or a clubbing in the dark of night.

Og needed a plan to earn the chief's trust or at least ease his fear of losing power. Og was reasonably confident that his leader would not take any direct action anytime soon. He put the problem aside while he contemplated ways to solidify the reality of his conjured spirits.

He gave spirits names and identifying symbols. The first named was Ura, the bringer of storms, and his symbol was a bolt of lightning. A spear symbolized Ka, the spirit of the hunt. A battle-ax represented Ra, the lord of war. He drew the symbols on the walls of his nearly barren and lonely cave.

Furthering his plan of continuing indoctrination, Og awoke every morning to speak to the day's hunting party to wish them well. He invented rituals and incantations with the intent to bolster their confidence. Sometimes he accompanied the party into the wild, knowing that his experience may make the difference between success and failure. He suggested that one of the younger hunters climb the tallest tree to look for game. That tactic was easier than looking for spoor on the ground.

Og's hunting and stalking skills, acquired and honed through the years, combined with the encouraging words assured fruitful hunts. The tribe's prosperity grew with each successful outing leading to more food, skins, and furs. After every hunt, whether or not he accompanied the hunters, the day would end with the priest lauding Chief Olo's leadership skills while offering thanks to his growing cadre of supernatural beings. His intent was to show that the chief's actions were as necessary as the gods' influence. As time passed, he created other spirits and claimed each had a specific function or duty.

Og did not perceive any change in Olo's unsubstantiated fears and believed that mere words of praise were not enough to allay his leader's apprehension—despite the fact that no one, not even the chief, could deny that the tribe was prospering of late. No doubt Og was also doing well. His formerly impoverished cave home was now decorated with wall art honoring his growing collection of imagined gods. His supply of necessary items increased on a daily basis. Og was sure that he would never go hungry again.

After feeling assured that his priesthood was established, Og made it a practice to leave the village during the full moon to "commune with the spirits," or so he told whoever asked. He had previously discovered a small cave in a hill near the village that he had furnished with sleeping mats, food that did not easily spoil, a spear, and a club. The little rock shelter became his home away from home. It was well supplied with basic necessities and was safe from the night-stalking predators.

One morning after a full moon, Og had not yet returned to the village when the hunters left. Chief Olo chose to accompany the party on that foray. On the trail of a big elk, the warriors interrupted a bear trying to dislodge a huge beehive from a low-hanging branch. The bear turned on the men as spears flew. Although three missiles struck the wooly beast, they did not stop it. It had enough life left to strike Olo on the thigh, opening a gaping wound. The chief was fortunate that the force of the blow also sent him flying, creating distance between him and the enraged beast. This gave the hunters some room to maneuver and hurl another volley of spears. That time the shafts did their job and downed the giant animal for good.

The hunters whooped it up, but their rejoicing suddenly stopped when they saw their leader lying in a pool of blood. Four of the strongest hunters picked up the stricken chief and carried him back to the village. The remainder of the troupe stayed behind to butcher the bear and carry it home in pieces.

Back in Olo's cave, his mate and other women did their best to stop the bleeding and wrap the thigh with medicinal leaves. They wished that Og was there because he was more skilled in the healing arts, and they believed he could entreat the gods to intervene. Og did not return until the next day. He had chosen to take a little longer rest from the ordeal of pretending he was the voice of the spirits.

On arrival, Og examined the wound and saw that it was already festering with infection. His people did not know that the claws of cave bears and other predators were often contaminated with bacteria laden remains of previous kills. Og did not know why infections happened but was instinctively aware that injuries became more severe when not kept clean. While he worked on the chief, he listened to the story of the attack, and his ears perked up when the speaker mentioned the beehive.

"Go quickly!" he said. "Bring the beehive, and do not lose a drop of honey. Run as fast as you can." Og knew of the healing benefits of honey. His mother had treated his father with honey when he'd had a serious infection many years ago. The remedy had worked then, and Og hoped it would work now.

The priest, now turned medicine man cleaned the wound thoroughly. When the honey arrived, he smeared it into and around the wound. Og then wrapped it with large leaves and tied them around the thigh with woven grass ropes. He told Olo's mate to give him plenty of water and to send for him if his forehead got hotter. Og did not forget to add a few incantations to the healing protocol even though he was the only one who knew that no amount of prayer could repair a wound, much less, that there were actual spirits listening.

For the next several days, Og spent much of his time attending to the ailing chief. He cooled him off when the fever went up and changed the honey-drenched dressings once a day. Each time he worked on the injury, Og mumbled some gibberish or rattled the bones he now carried in a little sack. The chief's younger sister, named Su, became his assistant while caring for Olo.

Although Og was ancient when compared with other tribesmen, some of the females who'd previously ignored him had begun to seek his company. He had been unaccompanied for a long time after outliving two mates. Now, working with Su gave him hope that perhaps she may find him desirable enough to become his mate. His hopes materialized into reality.

Og knew that everything he did would work either in his favor or against him when dealing with Olo's fear of losing control of his tribe. He had no desire to lead a tribe; that was far too much work and responsibility. He would rather tend to the people's spiritual needs, regardless of the validity of such needs. Olo had to survive and return to his duties as leader of the families. That would be the most important step in getting the chief to accept him for what he was: a priest with no desire to displace him at the head of the clan. The second biggest step was to solidify his relationship with Su. The mating would make Og a member of Olo's family, perhaps further easing the chief's concerns. Su's relation to Olo was not the only consideration. The woman was young, quite intelligent and eagerly absorbed Og's lessons on healing and at times, she joined him in the made-up incantations. She smiled suspiciously, perhaps knowingly at Og during his rituals.

Og continued caring for his chief until he was sure that the infection was gone and that his recovery was certain. By the next moon, Olo was well enough to walk with the assistance of his young son Ato and a sturdy staff. Olo would always be somewhat suspicious of Og, or maybe it was just jealousy. He also realized that Og could have let him die or even poisoned him. But now he was still alive and had to be grateful to Og for his efforts. The recovering chief was also well aware that the village had been prospering since the priest had started to seek the help of the spirits. Now, with his sister by Og's side, Olo was sure that betrayal was impossible.

There was no formal wedding celebration, vows, or betrothal ritual. Most matings happened naturally, when couples found each other mutually acceptable. Olo approved, and the couple joined to form a home of their own. Some of the other women who had designs on Og were disappointed and gossiped among themselves, but because Su was the chief's sister and was now under the protection of the spirit guide, they had no choice but to accept things as they were.

Olo's apprehensions diminished over time, to the point where Og was no longer concerned for his position or his safety. Whatever Og was doing worked in the eyes of the chief, the elders, and the village population.

The chief and tribal leaders began to invite Og to join them when they met to deal with village affairs or when it was time for important decisions. Og's wisdom became apparent, and his position and influence grew in importance. He was very careful to offer his thoughts as mere suggestions, not orders or demands.

The old man, now a fully anointed priest and adviser, was no longer alone after selecting Su as his third wife. Life was interesting again. He had no need to hunt or gather fruits and nuts in the field. His days were devoted to inventing spirits to honor—or conversely, to blame for inexplicable or tragic events. Su did her part. She never questioned the reality or fiction of her mate's spirit companions. The couple were happy and had no unfulfilled needs.

Each new spirit also received a name and identifying symbol. Even the newly created evil spirits received symbols. The chief dark spirit, represented by the moon, was named Lun. The snake symbolized the bringer of disease and received the name Hisa. Og was running out of space on the walls of his cave. He needed a bigger cave or would have to stop creating new spirits to worship or instill fear.

One day, Su asked her mate if the spirits had a leader or chief. Og thought quickly and said to his wife, "Of course. I just need a place of honor on my wall to draw his symbol." It did not take long for Su to contribute to the family business by naming the spirit chief and come up with a proper symbol. The most prominent feature in the sky is the sun. It can be the symbol of the greatest of spirits. She called him Alu and chose the sun as its sign.

Og was proud of his new wife and grateful that she had accepted him as a mate. He thought it best to have a ready answer if other members of the tribe asked about other spirits, their origin, and their purpose. He considered all the natural occurrences that required a spirit. There had to be more; surely one spirit, or just a few, could not be in charge of everything. Og also invented origins for the strange beings who managed the affairs of men and their world.

Another question that would someday need an answer was "How or why did the spirits create man?" Surely the gods must have come before people. Og took his time pondering the possible origins of his people. For now, simply saying the gods formed man out of the earth would have to do.

C H A P T E R 3

OG'S FAMILY PROSPERS

Within two years, Su produced a son, whom they named Tor, and a daughter named Nia. Og's devoted and skilled mate wanted to contribute to the fortunes of her family, and she learned to carve icons out of antlers, bones, and mastodon tusks representing her mate's cadre of spirits. She traded the icons for the shiny metals found in the river and in some caves.

Life was pleasant for Og and his growing family, but all was not well all the time. There were some difficult days on occasion. Og blamed unpleasantness on the dark spirits or, more effectively, the unacceptable actions of villagers. Redemption always came at a price. A speared bird or a fine pelt could satisfy the offended spirit and gain forgiveness for the misbehaving person.

Og knew that his children would be well off for the rest of their lives, or at least for as long as he held power, but he insisted that Tor learn to throw a spear and stalk game just as well as the other boys in the tribe. Og chose Ato, the clan's best hunter and son of Chief Olo, to mentor his son. Tor would have the best teacher, and Og gained an ally by selecting the grateful future chief as his son's teacher and protector.

Tor also had to study at home to learn about the spirits, their functions, and their origins. Og expected his son to carry on the family tradition when Og's time on earth ended. The bright boy absorbed every lesson his father taught him. The relatively rich life he enjoyed served as encouragement. He realized that the life of a priest offered more benefits, riches, safety, and ease than hunting or fighting.

Og's daughter was beautiful and just as bright as her brother and father. Nia became as skilled in carving figures as her mother and learned the lessons necessary for survival. She added the art of shaping the shiny metal from the river into ornaments that the villagers craved. The thought of teaching his daughter about the gods or spirits did not enter Og's mind at the time. An awakening would come later when fear of attack made them consider the number of warriors in the tribe and his daughter asked, "Why not me or the other women?" A notion further emphasized by the feistiness of a granddaughter not yet born.

Og's power and influence expanded as the people's belief in his alliance with the spirits grew in intensity. The chief always experienced a little jealousy, even after Og saved his life, but he was unable to fully comprehend the extent of the priest's power and remained too fearful to challenge Og's relationship with the mysterious higher powers. Tor flourished as an apprentice and studied his father's incantations and rituals while adding some of his own. Instinctively, he also suspected that the old man had invented the unseen beings and that his communication with them was purely imaginary. However, the young man was not about to let the secret escape.

Despite Olo's remaining jealousy, he was still content that his tribe was doing well. His hunters went out daily after receiving encouraging words and blessings from Og or Tor. Unsuccessful hunts were rare. It was not the hunter spirit's fault if a clumsy hunter cracked a twig or stumbled while stalking and scared away the targeted game.

CHAPTER 4
THE COMING OF WAR

Problems arose when nearby villages realized that Olo's people were much better off than they were. Jealousy turned to anger, which eventually led to skirmishes and raids. Previously, Og had not had any reason to invoke the war spirit, Ra. Now was a good time to exploit the war god's wrath and punish the unfaithful and rebellious clans. He and Tor met secretly to discuss a plan of action designed to embolden and encourage Olo and his warriors to teach other villages a lesson.

The village that caused the most trouble became the first target. Og believed that if the assault was effective, other villages would refrain from future challenges. The plan presented to Chief Olo and the elders included the rationale that other tribes could not be allowed to attack whenever they wanted without expecting strong retaliation. Og said, "We have fine warriors and Ra, the war spirit, on our side. Ato is also a skilled fighter and excellent leader. Those assets and a good battle plan will assure victory. Every village will hear of our success and will not dare continue their annoying acts of disrespect and violence." Chief Olo, his son, and all in the council agreed that Og's argument made sense.

Og decided that despite the danger and his youthfulness, Tor must accompany the warriors in battle. Nothing inspired more, or built greater confidence than the presence of the war god's representative in the conflict. Og instructed Tor to remain close to Ato and his favored warriors because that would be the safest position among combatants. The father and son team devised primitive shields emblazoned with a drawing of an ax, the accepted symbol of the war spirit. The icons would serve as a constant reminder of the deity's support.

On the day of battle, the predawn preparations included pleas from Og and Tor directed at Alu, the chief of the gods, and his son Ra for a victorious day. Blessings and encouragements, followed with the sacrifice of small animals, concluded the pre-battle ritual. Smeared with the sacrificial blood, the warriors marched off to battle.

Og was not only a talented priest but also a gifted tactician. He insisted on an early morning assault, when the enemy was still asleep or drowsy; they would be confused by the surprise attack. He also told the chief that the spirits needed blood offerings early in the day.

Ato's forces surrounded the target village with instructions to approach as silently as possible. The village dogs would likely sound the first warning, but that was not avoidable. The barking dogs were the signal to attack. As Og had advised, Tor remained close to Ato and his closest followers. The battle was brief but effective. The attackers' intention was to strike fear and not to kill indiscriminately. Og made every effort to convince Olo that it was better to have allies instead of eternal enemies. Killing for minor offenses might create unforgivable hatred. The raid was an immense success even though only a small number in the subject village died. Only a few of Olo's warriors were injured, and none seriously.

The invading party gained much treasure, including weapons, food, furs, and several young women. Appropriating females and adopting them into their own tribes was an accepted practice. Although oblivious to genetic factors, they understood that continuous inbreeding was not beneficial. Og was proud of his son, whose stature rose as both warrior and priest. His leadership qualities became apparent when suggesting the posting of permanent guards so that their own village avoided a similar setback in the future. They soon realized that other villages did not dare attack, and in order to keep the peace, many brought gifts to Olo and offerings for Og's assortment of deities.

Olo put aside his jealousy, and he finally accepted that it was best to remain on friendly terms with the priest and his ever-increasing following. As a result of Olo's actions and Og's influence, warriors and their families from other villages asked to join his now highly respected and feared group. Olo's clan would benefit from an infusion of new blood, guaranteeing continued growth for Og's congregation of followers.

CHAPTER 5
CHIEF ATO

In moments of quiet reflection, Og examined his present conditions. He was rich beyond his dreams, not only in material wealth but also in respect and honor. Despite the unprecedented success, he believed his greatest accomplishment was not the creation of an imaginary belief system, but producing a family of children and grandchildren who added so much to the pleasures of life. His immediate family grew, and he welcomed the arrival of more progeny with whom to share his knowledge and power. His goal was that they and their offspring would one day spread his teachings to other villages, and all people would come to accept the gods he had created.

Ato assumed leadership after his father, slowed by age and previous injuries, got too close to an injured and enraged mastodon. The village mourned for several days. Og and Tor led the tribe in rituals meant to guide the dead chief to the spirit world. He had been obedient and faithful to the spirits, who would surely welcome him. They buried Olo in the fetal position, signifying a new birth. His personal weapons joined him in the tomb.

Tor found a mate in Tia, one of Ato's daughters. As the son and daughter of the most prominent tribal members, the couple enjoyed a rich existence, yet they did not abuse their status. Tor still functioned as Og's assistant and continued to participate in hunts and raids. Tia learned the art of carving spirit symbols from Su and Nia.

Tor and Nia gave Og several grandchildren. The boys studied the spiritual teachings of their grandfather and the art of hunting and war from their father. Og impressed upon them that nature and fortune favored the wise and adept. The more they learned, the better off they would be. The girls were not ignored; they too learned the skills necessary for females of their era and even surpassed them. Lia, Tor's oldest, absorbed her grandmother's lessons and practiced the art of healing using herbs and potions.

His youngest daughter, Mina proved to be quite different in ways that would someday make her stand out among all other children. She learned to walk and talk faster than any of the others had and displayed an affinity for activity and adventure. And preferred playing with weapons instead of the toys made by her parents. Although she could barely lift it, her favorite plaything was her father's battle axe.

C H A P T E R 6
STRANGERS

One day, Tor chose to explore areas far from his village. He told his family that he would be gone for a long time, but not to worry. Og told the villagers that his son was on a journey to commune with the spirits in a quest to become a better servant.

Tor traveled in the direction from where the sun rose. To return, he simply needed to keep the rising sun to his back in order find his way home. He journeyed for many days, moving only during the day and securing himself in a cave or a tall tree when the sun went to sleep. He planned to walk as far as possible until the moon went from a sliver to full.

The exploratory trip was exceptional only in a few encounters with wild beasts that hunted him instead of the other way around. He escaped unscathed and even managed to kill a smilodon. Tor took the skull and fur as trophies, but he was wise enough to realize that the saber-toothed cat was slowed either by injury, disease, or age. Otherwise, he would not have had a chance by himself.

On the morning after the full moon, it was time to return home. He abandoned the perch in the tree and prepared to head back. A flume of smoke a short distance away captured his attention. Curiosity got the best of him, and he went to investigate. Tor was a skilled tracker and hunter, able to sneak up as silently as the blink of an eye on unsuspecting prey. He went into stalking mode as he approached the source of the smoke.

The sight he encountered almost drove him to carelessness. He caught his breath and continued to observe. In a clearing around a fire were some strange creatures, nearly like him but not quite. They had two legs and arms but smaller heads, and they were less hirsute. They wore strange garments as well.

He saw some carrying spears, as he did, but other men also carried an oddly bent stick tied at each end with a thin rope and a narrow container full of short, thin spears. His father had always told him not to be careless and to be wary of the unusual, but he could not go back home with just half a story. He needed to learn more about the strangers and their mysterious trappings.

He followed them cautiously but always maintained a good distance from them. Tor saw a herd of elk in a clearing at about the same time the outlanders did. They were near the herd but not close enough to hurl their spears, yet they did not attempt to get closer. A meticulous observer, Tor followed every move they made. Some of them reached into the narrow baskets and pulled out the little, spear-like sticks. They then joined them with the bent sticks tied with string. The hunters pulled back on the strings. The stick attached to strings bent even more. The men let go of the string, it snapped, and the sharp thin sticks flew nearly silently toward the elk. Three animals went down, and the odd people jumped from their hiding place to collect their kills.

"It is a weapon," Tor realized. The little sticks were as deadly as a spear, but they flew faster and from farther away. This meant less danger to a hunter or warrior.

Tor needed to learn more. He delayed his return home to follow the hunters and study them. He stayed near them for three risings of the sun. Sometimes he was close enough to hear them talk, but the strange sounds coming from their mouths were gibberish to him. He observed their hunting methods and watched carefully as they used their fascinating weapons. He collected some of the abandoned sticks that did not hit their targets and watched as the men made new ones. He had to have more of them to take back to his people. On the third night, as the unusual men slept, Tor crept into their camp and picked up one of the bent sticks and a basket of the sharp and deadly sticks.

He did not know whether they would notice or care if one of their weapons went missing, but he did not want to be near if they did. By the time they woke up, Tor would be very far away. He also made sure he did not leave an easy trail for them to follow. No one pursued him. It would be a long time before their tribes would meet again, and the result would affect both tribes forever.

Tor's return trip took a lot less time. He was anxious to get home and tell his father about the new lands and the strange people he had encountered. He needed his father's wisdom to determine whether or not to be concerned.

Tor hid the newly discovered items before entering the village. His father was better equipped to decide what, if anything, to tell the tribe. One thing was certain: his people needed to learn how to make and use the killing sticks if they were to survive.

Everyone was overjoyed at his return. A great feast, headlined by a large boar that Tor had brought with him, celebrated his arrival, and only the children got much sleep that first night. Tor limited his stories to describing the land and waterways he discovered and his private discourses with the various gods. His father would be the first to hear about the strangers and the amazing new weapon. He planned to go for a walk with Og the next morning, to talk to him privately about what he had seen and show him the wondrous tools he'd discovered.

The only sad moment came when Og admitted that his time above ground was coming to an end. "Son," he said, "the last half of my life has been greater than anyone could hope for, but I cannot continue much longer. It is so easy for me to tell the people that they should not fear death and that the spirits have a place for them. It is much more difficult to convince myself of the statement's validity because I am the one who made it all up. I'd like to believe, but …"

"Father, it is possible that there is more to come after we pass on. I knew almost from the beginning your stories were made up but I helped make believers out of our tribe and others. However, over the years, after repeating the same stories so many times, I may have even persuaded myself of that potentiality. It is time to assure yourself of the possibility, even if only to make your remaining days happier and more hopeful. However, it is not the time to talk about the end, but rather about a new beginning, after I show you what I found."

Tor showed Og the weapons he'd stolen from the peculiar-looking huntsmen. "Father, on the way back, I practiced what I saw them doing.

I missed the target more than I hit it, but I missed less as I tried more often. I even used the weapon to kill the boar I brought into the village just before I arrived. The people who made these also missed sometimes, just as our own best hunters miss with their spears. It will take a lot of practice to improve."

"Did these people see you?" Og asked.

"No. I did not get close until the last night, and they were asleep when I took these things."

"Good. However, we must remain on guard from now on. Just as I suspect they are dangerous; they may see us the same way. Their tribe may be bigger than ours, and they have better weapons."

"Yes, but now we have them too!"

Og said, "True, but they have more and are better skilled at using them. Did you see how they made them?"

"Yes. I watched them for days. I know the trees they chose for the bent sticks and the trees they used for the little flying spears. The tips are made the same way we make our spears, except smaller. We will have to examine the feathers on the other end to understand how to attach them. Mother is good at making trinkets for our people and toys for the little ones; she may see things we do not. That gooey stuff they make from the birch tree may come in handy too. Maybe it's the same way she used it to attach the points to our spears."

"The story we will tell them, son, is that the spirits rewarded our village with a new weapon, and we must learn to make them and use them properly. Remember, Tor, always give credit to the gods for anything difficult to explain, and to blame the actions of the people when something goes awry. The spirits may get angry and vengeful, but they are never wrong. Now, let us return to the caves and introduce our people to the new weapons. Starting tomorrow, take some of the warriors to the field and begin their lessons. Do not mention the strangers; it may frighten them too much. We can wait for the right time."

C H A P T E R 7
THE BIG CAT

Tor found the right trees to use for duplicating the new weapons. Su, Nia, Tia, and Lia studied the two pieces, and through trial and error, they produced working copies. As Tor suggested, the birch glue was very effective in attaching the small points and feathers. In a few weeks, ten warriors wielded the strange new arms. Gaining proficiency in their use was another matter. Only six, including Tor and Ato, could hit their targets with any frequency, even after many days of practice.

Tor and Ato wanted to test the weapons in a real hunt. They and four more adept archers plus two skilled spear throwers formed the party. They planned to go after deer or elk first because taking down a mastodon or bear with puny sticks seemed impossible.

They found a herd of deer quickly enough and positioned themselves in a semicircle around the target animals. There was another stalker that the hunters did not see, hear, or smell. The big longtooth noticed the new prey that was slower and less agile than deer or elk.

The cat singled out its target and charged with a loud roar. The terrified hunter froze in his tracks, and with no more than a whimper, he dropped his weapons and accepted his fate. Ato and Tor, with the advantage of experience and fearlessness, stepped out into the clearing, notched their sharp sticks, and let fly. Both found their mark. Tor's stick struck the panther's chest, but Ato's stilled its heart. The magnificent beast fell dead just a few steps from its intended prey. Tor approached the trembling man and told him to thank Ka, the protector of hunters. The other men were amazed at the skill of their leaders and even more so at the effectiveness of the diminutive spears hurled by the bent stick. They swore to the chief and the son of the priest, and of course Ka, that they would practice for as long as it took to match Tor and Ato.

22

C H A P T E R 8
FEMALE WARRIORS

The tribe did not particularly relish the meat of the big cats, except under unusual circumstances, but the hide and fangs were valuable. Two hunters stayed with the carcass to strip the longtooth of its hide and to sever the head. Tor and Ato would divide the prizes. The rest of the pack continued to track the scattered herd and put down two deer, which was enough to complete the village's evening meal.

The topic around the evening's fire centered on the bravery of the two cat killers and the wondrous weapons the spirits provided. From the next day on, the hunters spent every waking moment practicing to gain the skill necessary to take down any prey. In a few months, every warrior carried an arc and a handful of flets, as the weapons came to be called. Many of the women learned to use them too; some were even better at hitting targets than the men. Og had insisted on allowing the females to learn, but he did not say why at first. In the back of his mind, an idea was taking root. He'd always believed that the females were capable of doing more than having babies or scraping skins to make them wearable. His own daughters and granddaughters had showed remarkable skills in areas that men found difficult. A more urgent need became apparent with Tor's discovery of a possible new threat. Og felt that arming the women gave the tribe a better chance at survival in a battle where they could possibly be outnumbered.

Other villagers asked about the arcs and flets, but for now, they were not permitted to have them or practice with them. Og secretly told Chief Ato about the strangers Tor had come across during his foray into the wilderness. As a precaution, the village now kept four warriors on nightly watch on the perimeter of the village, which had grown in numbers and area. The watchers on duty did not hunt the morning after their turn but were rewarded for their work with an equal share of the hunt. Og also planted the seed in Ato's head that female warriors could be useful if attackers outnumbered the village men.

CHAPTER 9
OG PONDERS DEATH

"Father, when I returned from my journey, you said that your time was coming to an end. Why?"

"I am old. Have you ever seen anyone in any village as old as I am?"

"Not that I remember, but that does not mean you have little time left."

"I feel it. I am tired. I know it is coming soon, and I must make sure that you and your children are ready to continue. I do not want anyone to be shocked or surprised, and so I will tell Chief Ato that I expect to join his father and the spirits very soon, and that I choose the day, whenever it comes. Never display weakness or lack of control. You are a servant of the gods, and so you must be stronger than your followers and not subject to their frailties. One more thing: teach your children well. When you feel they are ready, send them to other villages to continue our work there. The gods belong to all the people, not just to our tribe."

"Father, you talk as if you truly believe the unseen lords are real."

"That does not matter. It is only important that the common folk believe. Our tribe has done well since the day they began to follow my teachings. Our people have prospered, and so have we—perhaps more so. Will you deny your children and theirs the riches and comfort our revelations have produced?"

"No. My family and I have lived well. We never go hungry. We work hard at what we do, but not to exhaustion. We are as powerful as the chief is, maybe even more so. We enjoy respect and honor. What more can we ask for?"

"Fear, my son. They must be kept afraid of what happens if they fail to be faithful, or if they ever think of turning against us."

"Yes, Father, I know. But their main fears are hunger, bad weather, raids from other men, sickness, and attacks by longtooths or dire wolves."

"Add this to their fears. In a dream, I saw dark, evil gods fighting with those we praise, trying to steal the essence of the dead and punish them for their misdeeds and for not worshipping them."

"So now there are malicious spirits too."

"I have hinted about them before, but not in detail. We have even named some of them, yet we have not emphasized their function or importance to us. Does it not make sense? There are sunny days and stormy days. There are daylight and nighttime. There are good plants that heal and poisonous ones that kill. We have good and bad people. We banish or kill the bad ones, but still others eventually appear. If everything in our world has opposite elements, then the gods must also have them."

Tor said, "We have led them to believe that there is some kind of existence after death. Why not emphasize that a terrifying experience waits for them if they do not live by the rules we give them? We will not punish them directly but threaten they will not meet their ancestors or walk with the good spirits after death. They will be taken by the dark gods to a place they can never leave."

"Good concept, son. Let's take a few days to solidify our story and think of some names and symbols for the hateful spirits. For now, let us worry about real threats and not the unseen, unproven ones. We have guards posted during night but have not concerned ourselves with daytime approaches, when an attack is more likely. You know that no one, no matter how brave, would dare challenge the cats or other meat eaters that hunt only at night. Seek a solution to that problem, and let me worry about the dangers of the spirit world, which you know as well as I do are extremely unlikely."

"Yes, Father," answered Tor with a sly smile. "You take care of the hard work, and I'll handle the easy jobs."

C H A P T E R 1 0
ATU AND KOR

Tor, Ato, and two of their older sons sometimes climbed the highest hill and scanned the distance for any unusual activity. The two fathers decided to assign their sons to take turns as lookouts. The two boys were instructed to not tell anyone what they were doing or why. Tor had named his son Atu at birth, similar to his best friend's name. Ato returned the honor by choosing the name Kor for his firstborn. Their new duty was from sunrise to sundown every other day because Og had pointed out that no warrior was stupid enough to be out in the woods at night when the big cats prowled for food. The chief and warrior priest assumed the outsiders were just as cautious. Besides, even if the moon was full, no one could see far anyway.

Kor asked, "Do we light a fire to warn you if they are near?"

Atu laughed and said, "I don't think so. If we see the fire and smoke in the village, they will too and may hurry to investigate or run off."

Tor put a hand on his son's head and said, "That's right, son. No fire, no smoke, no warning yells. Run down the hill as fast as you can, and tell the chief, your grandfather Og, or any one of us. If none of us is around, wake the night guards and tell them. Whoever sees anything should also send a runner to find the hunting party. You two claim to be the fastest runners, so whoever is not on the hill that day will go warn the hunters."

Kor looked gloomy and upset on the way down from the hill. His best friend had laughed at him and embarrassed him in front of his father. Strange thoughts began to stir in his head.

Atu was not yet old enough to have his own hut or cave, and so he still lived with his father. When they arrived at their cave, Tor spoke to his

26

son. "Did you notice that Kor was unhappy? You laughed at what he said. He is the chief's son, and someday he may even become the leader of the tribe. You should be more careful."

"But what he said was stupid."

"Quiet! Don't ever let him hear you say that. It could be very dangerous to you and the rest of the family, especially if he gets to be chief. Your grandfather knows more than anyone else in the whole village, and because of what he teaches us, we may be smarter than the other people. But that does not mean we are better. Others can do some things we cannot. Isn't Kor a swifter runner than you?"

"Yes. I can never catch him."

"Does he laugh at you or call you names?"

"Well, no, but he may now."

"And you'll deserve it. However, just because you think a little faster than he can, that does not mean he is stupid, just like being a slower runner than he is does not make you less of a man. Do you understand?"

"Yes, Father. I'll be more careful."

CHAPTER 11
SEEDS OF CHANGE
FOR WOMEN

Tor and Og took more time to prepare their growing brood to assume their roles as spirit guides. As they became adept, they visited other villages to continue the indoctrination begun by Og. Lon, Nia's oldest son, was the first to take up with another village on a permanent basis as the spiritual leader. Og remained with him for two weeks until he was sure that his grandson gained respect. The young priest proved to be a master at his new profession despite his age. Tor and Og were so proud of the job he did that they sent Nito, Tor's second born, to be his apprentice.

Other than the ever-present concern over the possible threat of the strangers, life for Ato's people was pleasant for a change. The forays for game were bountiful thanks to the increased skill of the hunters with the arcs and flets. The people in other settlements, especially those that began to follow Og's teachings allied themselves more with Ato's village. Because of that, Og encouraged trade with other tribes, allowed them to have some of the new weapons, and advised all warriors to practice. The thought of Tor's encounter with the apparently advanced tribe moved him to encourage and maintain friendly and peaceful relations with the outlying villages.

While exploring with his son, Og noted, "It is not right that your sister and my granddaughters can't be accepted as servants of the gods."

"I know, Father. They are smarter and more capable than most of the men in the village. Remember the problem we had convincing the warriors that it would be a good idea for the women to practice with arcs?"

"I have a job for you. I will not survive this generation, but you probably will. Find a way to teach future offspring that women deserve more respect and the freedom to make choices."

"That is a difficult assignment, but I will do my best. We can start with our own children. By the way, some of the clans outside our village consist of only a few family members. The group's oldest male usually takes charge but is not really a chief. They need spiritual guidance too. I have an idea. Why not send a visiting apprentice to instruct them on their religious needs?"

Og said, "Send two, your son Nito and daughter Lia, but only for a few hours a day and to a different family or clan several times a week. Make sure at least two warriors accompany them each time they go out. This will serve two purposes: the clans will get a spiritual education, and the notion of women as priests gets a start."

"Father, your goal is to keep control of our beliefs within the family, right?"

"Yes, son. For now, no one else can be trusted to use the power we have without abusing it. Maybe someday, as the numbers of followers increase, we may have to include others, but now is not the time. Let's keep it among family members and enjoy the benefits as well as the responsibility it carries for as long as possible."

CHAPTER 12
REVENGE

Atu noticed that Kor did not speak to him much anymore. He assumed that Kor was still upset for being laughed at, but he also believed that his friend would get over the slight eventually, and they would be friends again.

Some days passed, and on a day that it was Atu's turn on the hill, he heard a rustle of leaves and turned toward the sound. As he turned, a rock hit him on the head and knocked him to the ground. When he recovered his senses a few minutes later, he noticed blood on his forehead. He was also sure that Kor had thrown the rock even though he hadn't seen him. The injury was not severe enough to abandon his post, and he waited until sundown to return home and have a talk with his father.

When his day's chore ended, Atu rushed home. His mother cleaned the laceration and applied medicinal plants to help it heal. The injury did not shock the boy's mother. The village people lived dangerous lives and suffered many mishaps from falls, attacks by wild animals, and even fights among themselves.

When Tor returned from his day out, he questioned his son. "You know Kor did this, but you did not see him."

"Yes. I was facing away when I heard the approach. I thought it was a predator and reached for my spear. The rock hit me as I turned to see what it was. Animals do not throw stones, and Kor is the only one who may have a reason to hurt me."

"I agree, but we cannot accuse if no one saw him do it. I will speak to Chief Ato but will not say we know who did it. You rest tomorrow and do nothing that may make things worse. Be alert at all times. Kor is very skilled with spears and arcs."

"Rocks too, it seems."

After the evening meal, Tor met with Ato to go over the day's events. He told his friend of the attack on Atu while up on the hill, adding that he did not see who threw the stone.

"Could it have been the strangers who snuck up on him? And if it was the enemy near the village, then could it happen again?"

"It's unlikely that it was the people we expect. They would not have left any sign they were near and would have gone back to get more warriors. Plus, they would not have used a rock."

"Tor, tomorrow when we head out for the hunt, I will leave the group, sneak back to the hill, and stand watch near the boys' posts. You know that I am the most silent stalker, and no one can see me hiding. If the rock thrower shows up, I will take care of him. I will not tell Kor, so that he will not be apprehensive. I will continue for a few days, just in case."

"Good plan, Chief, but it is best to capture him alive so that we can discover why, and if there are others like him in the village." Tor knew there were no others but did not want Ato to react too quickly and harm his own son.

Obviously, there was no attack the next day. When Atu's turn came up the following day, Ato continued the plan the two older friends had worked out. That day, both Ato and Kor would learn that sometimes plans did not follow the desires or expectations of the schemers.

Kor was even angrier after his initial strategy had failed. He did not really want to kill Atu, but he wanted to make him unable to work for a while and lose his position. The job would then belong to him alone, and if he saw the enemy first, he would be hailed as a hero.

Kor left the village at daybreak soon after his father left with the hunters. This time he took his arc, flets, and spear. He was not sure whether Atu was already en route, but it did not matter. He could still surprise him at the top of the hill or on the way. Kor was so excited in his quest that he did not see the glowing yellow eyes of the hungry lioness following him up the hill.

Atu was almost at the top of the hill when he sensed something or someone behind him. He took cover behind a large tree and prepared his arc to fire. He then heard the roar of a lion and saw Kor running up the hill. Kor was fast, but cats were faster—there was no way he would win this race. Kor tripped on the root of a tree as Atu stepped out from his hiding place and pulled back on the string. His aim was true but not true enough. It stuck in the side of the beast but was not a fatal blow.

The cat ignored the wound as a man in a hurry would ignore a stubbed toe, and it continued toward its prey still on the ground. Atu did not have time to use the arc again. He picked up his spear and rushed to intercept the attacking predator. At that moment, Ato came on the scene but was still too far to launch a spear and did not have enough time to notch a flet. His hunter's vision and experience took in the whole scene in one glance. Either Atu, his son, or both would be dead soon, and all he could hope for was to avenge them by killing the carnivore afterward.

Atu confronted the lioness head-on. The cat leaped, and Atu met it with his spear full on its chest. The spear snapped, and the lioness, although nearly dead, still managed to clamp its jaws instinctively on the boy's shoulder. Both boy and beast went down, and neither moved.

C H A P T E R   1 3
REGRETS

Ato lifted the animal's carcass off the boy as his own son got up and cried for the first time since he was a toddler.

"Stop crying and come help. What were you doing up here? It is not your day. I think we will have a lot to talk about later. Bring some clean leaves—he is bleeding badly."

Ato worked feverishly to stop the bleeding and sent his son to get help from the village. Kor ran faster than he had ever run before. His frantic yells inspired the men to move quickly. When the responders arrived, two men carried the still unconscious Atu back home. Ato also told two other men to carry the dead lioness down to the village. It was Atu's first lion kill. The skull, pelt, and honor would be his—if he lived.

Another runner went to look for the hunting party and give Tor the news about his son. Although they had only snared a small deer, they decided to abandon the hunt and accompany the grieving father back to the caves. There would be little to eat that night, but there would not be much of an appetite either.

After Atu was treated, the two lifelong friends, assured that he would survive, took a walk away from the village.

Ato spoke first. "Did you know it was Kor?'

"No. We suspected but did not know."

"Is that why you warned me not to kill first?"

"Yes. I did not want there to be a second tragic error."

"Thank you, my friend. Now, how do I handle this? You are soon to be the tribe's spiritual leader, and I am the chief. Yet our sons…well, my son hates yours."

"That may not be true anymore. They were best friends until my boy laughed at Kor. By the way, I did reprimand him, and he realizes he made a mistake."

"I remember. I told Kor not to worry about it, but I see I was not convincing enough."

Tor added, "I believe that both boys learned a lesson, and hopefully Kor's desire for revenge is fully satisfied."

Ato said, "Whether satisfied or not, after doing the same boring job every day, he will now see that having is not as desirable as wanting."

"I know, friend. But still, he is your son, and you can't punish him forever. Another boy needs to be trained when you feel that Kor has had enough."

"Tor, every time I look, Og has another grandson or granddaughter. Pick one of them."

"Good idea, Chief." Tor immediately knew who would be best suited to replace Atu on day watch.

CHAPTER 14
MINA

Atu was laid up for a few weeks while he recovered from the vicious bite. During that time, Kor had lookout duty every day. The monotony turned out to be a doubly boring job. Neither was it as honorable as he thought it would be. However, he was glad that the truth was not generally known. No one other than Ato, Tor, the two boys, and Og was aware of the sequence of events and the fact that Kor had previously injured Atu.

Kor also made sure to visit Atu every day after his duties on the hill. He begged forgiveness and vowed that Atu would be his friend for life, no matter what.

Atu recovered, but the injury would keep him from ever using an arc again. The weapon needed two good arms to work properly. He could still throw a spear, so he was not totally helpless. Besides, his future lay as a priest or spirit guide, and there would be no need for weapons other than his wits and imagination for that job.

After a month of daily monotony as hill lookout, Kor was charged with training a new guard. To Kor's surprise, the new recruit was Mina, Atu's younger sister. She was sharp-eyed and handy with an arc. Kor did not care that he had to share his job with a girl. He knew it was important duty and did not mind working every other day, but he was sick of the day after day drudgery. Mina also had the distinct honor of being the youngest member of the tribe to have single handedly killed a saber tooth tiger.

"Grandfather", she had asked Og, at a slightly earlier age, "If you say that I should be treated as my brothers and other boys are, why can't I learn to hunt or throw a spear?"

"Probably because I never thought that you might be interested. I am sorry for being ignorant or not asking. Now I see that I should have realized this sooner. I will ask Po, our best hunter to begin your training. Your father is just as good but his personal feelings may interfere with his enthusiasm or teaching methods."

"Not just with the arc, flets and spear. I want to practice with the battle axe too."

"Little one that will depend on what your mentor believes you are capable of."

"Ha! you'd be surprised of what I can do."

"But Mina, you will still be expected to continue your studies in the family business. Our family's main purpose is to speak for the spirits and show the villagers the way to better lives."

"Yes grandfather, but I wish that was one job that only the boys had to do."

"You will soon learn that under certain situations, words are more powerful than spears or axes."

Po could not refuse the high priest and eldest member of the tribe. The very next day he and Mina went to a clearing away from the village. Po did not wish to be seen training a girl, especially one as young as Mina.

He found the girl to be an apt student. She showed early signs of raw but innate skills. They began with the spear. Po believed that the shorter thinner spears meant to be thrown would be the perfect weapon for her. In a matter of a few days, she was on target more often than not. While she could not throw it as far as grown men, it was far enough and fast enough to be nearly as effective.

The thrusting spear was heavier but to be truly useful the wielder had to be closer to the target or prey, making it more dangerous and more difficult to manage due to her youth and diminutive build. The battle-axe required even closer contact with an enemy and required more strength to be useful in a real encounter. Practice would help her build muscle strength but Po suggested that it would be better to wait until she grew a little more before relying on the axe. The arcs and flets were another matter. All that was required was enough strength to pull back the string and a have good eye for aiming. With sufficient practice, this weapon in her hands could be as lethal as in the hands of any warrior, regardless of size.

She had an unexplainable fondness for the axe but understood her mentor's concern over her physical limitations in handling it.

The more Mina practiced with the arcs and flets the more she cared for it as her weapon of choice. Her second choice was the thinner throwing spear. The best weapons are the ones that kill from a distance, thereby keeping the user safer. She continued to practice with the thrusting spear and the axe because warriors need to have varied skills and backup weapons in reserve.

Before being chosen for hill duty, and not scheduled for training with Po, her parents or grandfather, she enjoyed venturing in the woods running free and exploring despite her parents' warnings not to go into the forest alone. She was fearless but had never encountered a dire wolf or any other dangerous creature when alone. As she cavorted, carefree in the forest, a low growl brought her senses to full attention. The young girl's heart beat faster but not out of fear. This was the first time that she had felt the full flow of adrenalin in her body. She felt strong but without weapons, no amount of strength could defeat the saber tooth just yards away. Mina thought quickly, the only available defense were the rocks of various sizes that littered the ground around her. She had thrown rocks before to knock down fruit high in trees but never at something that could kill and eat her with little effort. She picked up two that fit easily in her hands and hurled one at the big cat. She missed, but the second one hit the beast on the head but not hard enough to do any damage. She gathered and threw as many as she could in succession. Her hits annoyed it more than hurt it until one struck the tiger in one eye and drew blood. After a couple more hits, the cat turned and disappeared into the brush. Mina collected two more rocks, turned and ran back to the village faster than she had ever run before. She vowed that she would never again leave the village without weapons.

When her teacher heard the story, he chided her first for disobeying her parents, second for venturing out alone and third for not carrying at least a spear when exploring.

Resuming the lessons, Po said, "It is not only necessary to hit the target, but to hit it in the right spot. Even if your flet enters the chest, it may not stop it and could still retaliate and kill you even while in the process of dying. It cannot hurt you when dead but definitely can on the way to death. Do you understand?"

"Yes, Po. My flet must stop the heart. Even if I cripple a leg, it can still get to me."

"True, Mina. It is also more difficult to hit a moving target, so you must be agile enough to notch flets one after another as fast as you can in case the first one just wounds it or worse yet, angers it."

Po's comment about hitting a moving target made Mina stop and think on how she could gain the skill to hit moving targets as easily as stationary ones. After pondering the question for a little while, she constructed a bundle made of grass, leaves and twigs tied it with a rope made of braided grass, and using a rope made of vines, hung it on a low hanging tree branch. She then pushed it to make it swing back and forth and ran a short distance away. The young would-be huntress notched flet after flet and fired away as the target swung back and forth. At first, she missed every time. Undaunted, she practiced day after day until she figured out that the flet had to be aimed, not where the target was, but where it would be a second or two later. Her joy was virtually immeasurable after her first successful strike on the moving target. Mina's accuracy and rate of hits increased with each day of practice.

The future warrior had not yet shown Po her moving target invention. She wanted to wait until she had acquired enough skill for a meaningful demonstration. Mina picked a nice sunny day to show her mentor what she had done. She mounted the target on the branch, walked away about 20 paces and asked Po to push the bundle and to step away. Her first flet hit the pendulum-like target when it reached its high point on the left and again on the rise to the right. Po was impressed. He found out that it was not as easy as she made it look when he tried to hit the swinging target. He had hit moving targets before but mostly when the target was moving directly toward him in a straight line, such as an opposing warrior or charging prey. For a brief moment, Mina became the mentor and Po the student when she corrected his failed attempts.

Later that day Po met with Tor, Mina's father, to heap praise upon his daughter's progress and her increasing skill. Po also described the moving target Mina had devised and suggested that all warriors practice on similar targets. Tor said he would speak to the chief and explain the benefits of improving the hunters' skills.

Foolishly, according to her parents, but bravely, according to her own perception, Mina continued cavorting through the woods, sometimes with a friend, but more often alone. On one solitary venture, she again heard a low growl coming from a nearby copse of trees. Every one of her senses was instantly on the alert. She planted her spear in the ground beside her, un-shouldered her arc and notched a flet.

The fringe of tall grass surrounding the trees slowly parted and she saw the black nose, the six-inch fangs and the glowing yellow eyes of a saber tooth. She took a deep breath to steady her nerves planted her feet firmly and prepared for battle. She felt her heart beat faster, out of anticipation and the thrill of battle. She felt the sudden rush of adrenaline needed during the coming encounter. The tiger began to move slowly toward Mina. The steel-nerved girl noticed that the beast would carefully re-arrange her rear paws directly under her haunches with every step, gauging distance, and preparing for a leap.

Mina could not allow the cat to get close enough for it to make the jump. She pulled back the string and let her flet fly. The missile struck it right above the right shoulder, a solid hit, but not incapacitating enough. Mina prepared another missile as the beast took a few painful steps and attacked. The second shot hit it mid chest but its momentum did not slow. In one action Mina sidestepped, grabbed her spear and, as the saber tooth hit the ground right beside her, she plunged the javelin just above the animal's left shoulder. Mina moved away in case the cat had life enough left to strike at her with claws or fangs.

Mina held her breath, ready to take action if the beast moved. It did not. She approached, still warily and noticed an old injury over the tiger's left eye. It was the same long-tooth that had threatened her before. This predator would not hunt nor threaten anyone else again.

The carcass was too big for her to carry or even drag home. She did not want to leave it available to carrion eaters but in this case, she had no choice. The elated, now fully qualified hunter ran home to get help to take her catch home.

Her father had not joined the village hunters that day and had just finished conferring with Chief Ato about village matters. Mina was happy to see him as they arrived at their cave at about the same time.

"Father, you see that I am un-harmed, so please do not berate me after nothing terrible happened to me."

"What are you talking about, Mina?"

"I came across a saber tooth and killed it."

"What?"

"I came across…"

"I heard what you said, girl. I am glad you are fine; I just cannot believe my little daughter would kill a tiger before older boys. Some grown village men haven't either."

"Well, some have not had the opportunity yet. But father, I had to leave it out in the open. Need help to bring it back to collect the head and skin."

"Wait here, Po was at the meeting too. I'll get him, but he will not believe it either."

Not only Po, the chief and several others who had been in the vicinity and heard the unbelievable story joined the recovery party. Both father and mentor beamed with pride when they saw the result of Mina's training. The men made short work of removing the head and skinning the animal on the spot. They ate cat meat only when there was nothing else available and they left the stripped carcass for the scavengers.

Her mother and a few other females prepared the skin so that Mina would have a brand-new outfit. They also made a necklace of the two fangs for Mina to wear as a sign of her prowess. Mina mounted what remained of the skull above her sleeping berth. Her family had another exemplary member. Her grandfather was high priest and the oldest man anyone had ever seen. Her father was a great hunter-warrior and had provided the first arc and flets to the village. Atu had saved the chief's son. Now Mina was the youngest tribal member to have faced and taken down a saber tooth, and alone. Villagers had little else to talk about for days except for Mina's incredible feat.

The young hunter had never had a problem with village bullies because of her dominant attitude but now she could extend her aura of defiance and confidence to stop the bullying or harassment of any unfortunate who was perceived as "not belonging" and therefore a target for abuse.

She made it a point to befriend all, especially those felt left out due to a disability or any other real or imagined difference.

For the first time in tribal memory, a female was allowed to join the hunters. She did not go on hunting forays on a daily basis. She still had studies at home and later would have hill duty on alternate days. Mina was still a child and had other things to learn. Her father and grandfather wanted all the family children to study the names, duties and history of each spirit that the two high priests purported to speak for. Many of the children were expected someday to become priests in villages of their own.

During one of the discussions and spiritual indoctrinations with her father and brother, Mina said, "We always talk about male gods and spirits, and Alu is the father of most of them. I know that baby people come from mothers. Don't the baby gods need mothers too?"

"Yes Mina", said Tor, "They sure do, but it is a subject that never came up. It seems we needed a female point of view to see that flaw in our stories. Let us work on it. Alu's mate needs a name first. Mina, do you have any suggestions?"

"She has to be strong and in charge of something important in our world. Give her control of the trees, plants, flowers and everything that grows in the ground."

"Very good little sister." Said Atu. "How about a name?"

"Gia!" said Mina, "Her name is Gia. And her symbol is the evergreen tree since it survives even the coldest days."

"And you, my dear daughter will be known as speaker of the earth goddess Gia as well as tiger slayer." Said Tor.

The newly appointed priestess smiled broadly at her father's encouraging words. Even though Mina preferred the hunt and wielding weapons, she still instinctively understood that it was the family's spiritual legacy and duties that permitted her to enjoy a rich exciting life. No other youngster in the village outside her family had what she had, including a private hunting mentor that was not a parent, brother or uncle.

After taking over hill watch for her injured brother, Mina found it boring at times but the lonely outpost gave her plenty of time alone to practice with the heavy battle-axe. She discovered that it made a good throwing weapon as well as one for close encounters. She made every effort to practice with all combat and hunting tools in her arsenal. The relentless practice had already saved her in a life and death struggle with a predator and would come in handy in a greater battle with much more devious and dangerous opponents not too far in the future.

The young huntress also had plenty of leisure time to plan for or dream of more exciting exploits in her future. Two goals formulated in her mind. On, how can one hunter take down a cave bear? It has more weapons, claws, large teeth, agility, and can climb some trees. A mastodon is bigger but slower. Tod harm, it must be near you.

Much of her thinking while awake and not busy revolved around the mastodon plan. Finally, an idea blossomed. She was speaker for Gia. Why not let her imaginary goddess herself help?

On one of her days off from hill duty, Mina requested to be allowed to join the next Mastodon hunting party. When her father asked why, she simply said she wanted to see how it was done. She promised not to get too close or interfere with the other hunters.

The preferred method was to isolate one animal from the herd and hurl as many spears were necessary to bring it down and then the hunters used thrusting spears to kill it. Another tactic was to stampede the herd toward a cliff where many would fall to their deaths. It was effective but wasteful. More animals than were needed were slaughtered needlessly.

Mina watched from a safe distance as she had promised while three hunters approached the herd. Seven others stayed behind. The three lead men selected their target and got close enough to hurl spears or flets. The missiles were not enough to kill but meant to anger the beast so it would chase the men.

By design, the one they selected was not near the herd. They only wanted to anger the one, not the whole herd. As planned the angry bull went after the source of the pain. Two parts had to fall in place. The men had to make sure the beast was close enough to continue the chase but not near enough to catch them. When close to the other seven companions, they all attacked the now fatigued prey with volleys of spears and flets.

Mina watched with interest. She now knew how to isolate one animal from the group. She also had a good idea of how far she had to stay ahead of it. Taking it down to a vulnerable position was the dilemma. That's where the spirit earth mother lends a hand.

On the selected day for her adventure, Mina bundled flets, spears and a digging tool her people used to make holes in the ground. She left at sunrise and headed for the area the Mastodons were known to frequent. When sighting them and gauging a distance similar to the one used in the previous hunt, she dug a trench about as wide as her arm, as long as a man is tall and as deep as her knees. She then placed four spears at an angled position below the top of trench. The last step was to cover the opening with branches and leaves. She rested from digging as she watched the herd's activities and paid close attention when one animal strayed from the herd. By pure luck, the one that separated did so in her direction.

Well rested and anxious for real excitement, she moved toward her target, When close enough, she began to yell and wave her arms trying to get its attention. It ignored her attempts. Her first flet got its attention but it was more of a mosquito bite than an injury. The second hit a more tender spot but the follow-up spear really hurt. The majestic beast reared on its hind legs, trumpeted in anger and charged. Mina ran, glancing back making sure it was still coming but not getting too close. Mina leaped over the trench with the animal just yards behind. To her dismay, the plan did not work. The Mastodon missed the trap completely and was still charging. The fleeing girl made a sharp turn and went back the way she was coming from. The bull was not as agile and while attempting the same sudden turn broke its right front leg. It went down heavily causing more injuries. It flailed attempting to rise leaving its underside exposed, Mina, not so reverently, thanked her patron goddess and hurried to put the behemoth out of its misery.

It was a long trek back to the village and had time to plan something unusual. She arrived at her parent's cave where her mother asked why she was so dirty,

"I was trying to catch a Mastodon, or rather, it was trying to catch me."

"Mina, what am I going to do with you?"

"Well, if you insist, you can do something with me now. There is a huge pile of meat out there that needs to be brought home. The me always get the glory of providing for the tribe. Why can't the women do it today for a change?"

"I think I know what you mean, How many of the women will we need?'

"Most of them, Mother."

Two hours later, a caravan of women left the village after Mina told her father that she had a surprise for him, but she needed the women and to please make sure the men remained in the camp while they were gone. Tor had great confidence in Mina but even more so in his mate, Tia. He also had given up on being surprised by his daughter's antics; he deeply suspected that this was another of her unique and dangerous adventures.

On the way to collect the bounty, Mina detailed what had occurred. There would be no need to re-tell the story during the village's evening meal and celebration since all the men would have heard the tale from their mates, sisters, mothers, aunts, nieces, and other female fro=inds and relations.

Much later the troupe of women returned, burdened with enough meat for many days. It would keep longer now that the cold season was starting.

Og and Tor were concerned. Mina was exceptional but took too many chances. They would need to talk to her. The very next day, the three took a leisurely walk for a father-daughter-grandfather talk.

Mina spoke first – "I know what this is about. I'm reckless and someday I will pay for that. Just know that I planned every step of the hunt and even though it did no fall into my trap, the hunt was a success."

Tor followed with – "You may not be so fortunate next time and I is always better to have a companion in case something goes wrong."

"Yes father, but didn't you go on a long journey to nowhere in particular all by yourself?"

Og broke in- "She's got you there, son."

"Whose side are you on, father?"

"Neither, but I may point out errors in either side of the discussion."

Mina continued-"Okay, I admit that when it did not fall into the trench I prepared, I knew I had made a mistake. I did not tell anyone that I had made an error or that it was wrong to go by myself. And, by the way, the trench plan will work if it is made a little wider and longer. I did fix it a little by telling all the women that Gia saw my predicament and caused a tree root to trip my pursuer, saving my life."

The two men could not help but laugh. She had learned her lessons well.

"I promise I will not take any more reckless chances alone…after I get my first cave bear."

Now it was her turn to laugh.

CHAPTER 15
THE END OF OG

Og became less active in tribal affairs as Tor took over most of the village's spiritual functions. In addition, Atu increasingly became a prominent participant in rites and rituals. More of Og's grandsons followed his example. Five villages now had priests from Og's family, and other family members visited villages on a regular basis. The patriarch's main function was to hold reunions with his descendants every full moon to hear about their activities and sometimes offer advice. At one such reunion, the frail old man announced to his extended family that this would be his last audience; he would not be here when the moon filled again. The Og clan was neither saddened nor disappointed. They understood that all lives reached an end because of accident, war, illness, or, in Og's case, age. Og had done all he had to do, and it was time to move on. Despite the spiritual teachings they imposed on the villages, they were never certain themselves of what came after one took that last breath. They understood there was no way of knowing. Death was a natural, unavoidable fact.

They bid their farewells and thanked the ancient one for all he had done for them, and then they moved on with their lives.

Three days later, Og summoned Tor, Nito, Atu, Nia, Lon, and Mina. He said, "Walk with me one last time, my children."

He had already selected where he would spend his last days. It was a nearby small barren mountain where villagers did not go because there were few caves and no sign of water or game.

"The first request is that you look after Su. She does not have much time either, but she is not quite ready. Bury her where you leave me today; I will not be far. You have been excellent students and even better sons, daughters, and grandchildren. No man could be prouder. Continue your work and make sure your children pass on what you teach them to their children and grandchildren. Tor, I do not know whether the strangers we worry about will hurt or help us. Whatever fate awaits our people, do all you can to maintain our culture and beliefs. They may need an introduction to our gods. Convince them, no matter how long it takes, that ours are better than theirs are, if they have any. I wish I had more time ahead of me than behind so that I could take part in whatever happens when the two people finally meet."

They arrived at the arid mountainside and looked for a shady spot to spend a few last comfortable moments together.

"Here is where I will stay forever. Help me dig a grave. You will not need to cover me; the elements will take care of that in time." They placed a few of his favorite possessions in the tomb and spoke of family matters and the future of their tribes.

In the last few years, summers had gotten shorter, and the winters were noticeably colder. They considered whether it would be best to move farther south, where they believed it might be more pleasant. Tor asked the ancient one if he should go again in search of the newcomers. "Yes," Og said. "Do not go alone; take Lon with you. He is a great stalker and hunter. Leave Atu in charge of our priestly duties; his injured arm hinders him in hunts and possible confrontations with the others."

"Should we greet them if found?"

"Not yet. Keep your distance and continue studying their ways. If they appear to be heading in the direction of the village, gather more warriors, but keep them hidden until the visitors discover you and your much smaller party. Judge their intentions. If hostile, signal the concealed warriors. Do not let any escape. Otherwise, they may return with a force you may find difficult to counter. Keep at least one alive so that you may learn more about them. It is preferable that the prisoner is a young one who is less wise and more manageable."

"I will do as you say. It is a shame that you cannot join us in this adventure. I do not really know these people, but I have a hunch that they would like you and appreciate your wisdom."

"I have had my share of adventures. You were not around to benefit from them. It is fitting that I not be around to interfere with yours. You have absorbed enough of my wisdom and developed your own. They will have to be content with what you offer them."

"Thank you for your guidance. It is time to go, Father. May you find what you expect."

"Son, I fear that what follows death may be what preceded birth… nothing. "I really do not expect much, but whatever it is, if anything, will be a welcome sight. Go now, before the beasts begin their evening hunt."

After speaking the last words, he would ever say to another living being, Og watched his children leave and sat on the edge of his newly dug grave to silently await the next phase of the cycle of existence, if there was one.

With the family gone, Og had the solitude that he often craved to not only rest but also contemplate on what he had done. It was not always to rejoice. He was definitely glad that he had provided well for his family and given them the tools to continue in prosperity, but he was not too sure of what he had done to, or for, other people. He wondered whether future generations of priests might distort his words and corrupt his intent. He feared they might use the powerful force of conviction solely for personal gain or to exert unjust control and power over naïve followers. His last wishes included a hope that his descendants would keep true to his teachings.

His preaching was sound and not meant to hurt anyone. Perhaps he simply presented a form of false hope that in reality was harmless, whether true or not. If the beliefs turned out to be true, the efforts were well worth it. If not true, and there was nothing after death, no one would ever know, and it would not matter. His self-satisfying redemption was that he had at least provided the people some comfort that there was no sudden perpetual nothingness after their last breath. He would like to share that comforting thought himself. It was extremely difficult for him to imagine the total extinction of thought or action just as there was absolutely nothing before a baby took its first breath. Those were his final sentiments as he closed his eyes and faded into oblivion.

C H A P T E R   1 6

STALKING THE STRANGERS

Tor and his nephew prepared for their quest. Tor added to his plan by relieving Kor of the hill-watching job, which had become tedious. Tor invited him and three other warriors to accompany them for a half moon's portion of the journey, where they would wait for their return or a sign that something had gone wrong. Kor selected a tall hill to set up camp and a point of observation. *Well, at least it is a different hill with a new view, and I am not alone,* thought Kor.

One of the four would always remain on the hill while the other three hunted or searched for water. The tall hill had a small cave that served as sleeping quarters, and a wind barrier of rocks and branches offered protection from the weather and predators. The young men settled in for what may turn out to be a long wait.

Back in the tribal home, Atu was now the chief priest in attendance, and he managed the religious side of the villages' activities and continued his younger brother's spiritual education. Nito was another apt student. He learned quickly and instinctively understood the nuances of his family's teachings. He knew it was all made up, but in his eyes, it did no harm and was actually beneficial in some ways, especially for their ever-growing family. Atu also made time to continue the education of his little sister, Mina, on days that it was not her day on the hill as an observer. Although he had an almost useless arm, he could still help her to become an expert in the use of bows and other weapons of battle. He also did not forget to instruct her in the main business of the family, the priesthood. The young girl preferred practicing the art of war, but did not reject her spiritual lessons.

Tor and Lon continued their search. This time they would travel farther than where Tor had first seen the strangers. They looked for signs of other camps or evidence of other visits to the area, and they found many. It appeared to Tor that this was a regular hunting ground, and it had expanded since his first encounter. Lon climbed the highest trees to look around every few miles. They did not want surprises.

One time he came down and excitedly said, "I saw a fire."

"Close enough to get near it before night comes?"

"Yes. They are not very far."

"We must travel now as if we were hunting for deer, slowly and very quietly."

"I will go first then, Uncle. I am a better stalker than you and have sharper eyes."

"For once I agree with you, but do not get overconfident. I'm still wiser and in charge."

"Yes, I understand. I did not mean to dishonor you."

The two moved out, silent as shadows and with every sense alert. Lon held up a hand, signaling stop. The camp was in sight. The strange visitors showed no sign of apprehension and acted as if they were as safe as in their own caves.

Og's son and grandson watched silently until it was no longer safe to be out in the open with darkness approaching. They expected the next few nights to be uncomfortable. They could not build a fire to ward off the nocturnal stalking beasts, and they had to sleep high up in trees.

In the early morning, they headed back to the hunters' camp. They wanted to determine whether the men planned to return to their land or continue ahead. Then Tor had to guess which way they planned to go. Tor did not see any stacked or hung carcasses and so decided the hunt was not finished. He and Lon circled the camp to find signs indicating from which direction the strangers had come. Lon's sharp eyes and natural stalking sense discovered they came from where the sun rose. Tor agreed and chose to watch from that direction because the party would not be returning that way any time soon.

This group had as many members as fingers on a man's hands. Tor also noticed which one was the apparent leader. He would be the one to focus the most attention on and the first to kill if attacked. He pointed the man out to Lon and said, "He is the one you aim your flets at first."

The hunters gathered their weapons, put out their fire, and moved in the opposite direction from the two watchers. Tor and Lon waited until their quarry was out of sight and chose this time to use the dying embers of the abandoned fire to lightly cook a rabbit they had caught the night before. It was their first cooked meal in many hours. The interlopers did not suspect any followers, and so the group made no effort to hide their trail. A blind man could have followed their path through the forest. Still, Tor and his nephew maintained extreme caution. If discovered and attacked, they would not stand a chance. Tor instructed Lon that his first priority was the safety of his people, not his uncle. He was to return as fast and as safely as possible, and leave Tor behind to slow the enemy for as long as possible. Lon was an excellent tracker and knew how to set up false trails. He was to mislead and delay any pursuer so that he would have time to reach and warn the village to set up a defense.

"Lon, do not get upset over what I tell you, even if repeated. I must make sure that you know what to do if I do not make it back. If I say something you already know, then accept it as reinforcement. If you do not, absorb it as a new lesson."

"I am sure we will both make it back, but I do enjoy your teachings, even if I've already heard them from Mother or Grandfather."

"Good. You are wise beyond your years. My sister has taught you well."

They continued in silent and careful pursuit, remaining just close enough to hear the men's strange tongue and observe their ways of hunting. These men were very accurate with their arcs and flets; they rarely missed. Tor also noticed that some hunters used a different tool. It was made of bone or wood about the length of a man's forearm, and it had a notch on one end where the tail end of the short spear fit. They called it an *atlatl* and used it to hurl a short spear farther than a longer one by hand. After a few days of careful observation, Tor and Lon added other new words to their growing vocabulary. Deer were called *cuvos*, and fire was *figo*.

When the hunters killed three deer and a small boar, they made litters—something new to Tor and Lon—to drag their bounty to wherever they came from. Tor surmised that their village could not be too far or the meat would spoil. He also judged that so much meat would feed a large village, and if they followed the same strategy as his own people, there were hunting parties in different directions, meaning it was an even larger settlement.

Along the way, the hunters built a lodge of sticks, grass, and skins and placed the skinned and gutted animals inside. They then lit a fire in the hut and covered the entrance. They kept the small fire going—not to cook the meat but to make more smoke. The action was unfathomable to Tor, but it was something he needed to understand.

Tor and Lon took a chance and stayed up all night, dozing off in shifts. They hoped the predators would not approach the humans because of the all-night campfires and the smoke escaping from the one hut.

At sunrise, the camp stirred. The men took the meat from the hut, wrapped it in large leaves, reloaded the litters, and resumed the return journey home.

"Are we going to follow them all the way?" asked Lon

"No. I do not believe they know we exist, and we do not know how long their return journey is. Next time we will prepare for a longer trip and follow them all the way. Kor may be getting impatient, waiting for so long. It is time to head back."

Once they had put some distance between themselves and the hunters' camp, Lon said, "Uncle, while you slept, I did something that may make you angry."

"We are still alive, so you were not caught doing whatever it was. What did you do?"

"I snuck into the camp and stole the thing they used to throw their spears farther than we can."

"You stole one of their weapons? You put us in danger, and I told you that the most important duty is to get information back to the tribe so that we can protect ourselves if they discover our village."

"Didn't you steal the arc and flets the last time?"

"You did well by getting the tool, but you were wrong to not tell me first. And I was alone then; I only put myself in peril. Also, it was Og and Ato who understood the real danger the strangers may pose. I was younger then and obviously as foolish as you."

"Yes, Uncle. I won't do that again."

"Did you pick up a short spear too?"

"Of course. The tool by itself is useless.

"Su, Tia, and your mother will be busy for a while making more of these things, and our hunters will have a new weapon with which to practice. I hope you watched carefully and understand how they work."

"I think so. As soon as we have more spears, I will practice. I do not want to lose the only one we have."

The two continued at a steady pace, stopping only for brief breaks to hunt, eat, and rest. Several days later, they reached the hill where Kor and the other men waited. Tor related their adventure and praised Lon for his skill and bravery. The one part he could not explain or understand was the placing of the meat in the smoke-filled hut.

Kor thought for a while and said, "The smoke must do something to the flesh. It must change it somehow. You know, like when the snows come: the food that is left in the cold does not rot as it does in the warm season. Maybe the smoke does the same thing to the flesh."

Lon said, "That's a good way of looking at it. They did not really cook it; they simply let it hang all night in the smoky hut. They ate some of it in the morning but cooked it first."

Tor agreed with both young men. "When we get back home, we can build a similar hut and see what happens to the meat we store after exposed to the smoke."

The journey back to their village took a few days less than the trip out. They were anxious to get a good rest in the comfort of their caves and fur berths. Kor and his crew of watchers on the hill had eaten well and had done little except hunt, eat, and nap. Tor and Lon were very tired from trailing the visitors, dealing with uncomfortable conditions, and not getting enough quality sleep while perched in trees.

The young man who had replaced Kor as lookout on the hill near the village spotted the returning party from far away. His duty was to notify the chief or anyone of some authority in the village. He ran as fast as he could down the hill and found Chief Ato resting after the day's hunt.

"Some men approach the village from there," said the young lookout, pointing east.

"How many?" asked Ato.

The boy held up six fingers.

"It has to be Tor and my son."

CHAPTER 17

PREPARING FOR THE STRANGERS

The chief gathered twelve men to accompany him. Fully armed, they marched out to meet the approaching group.

Ato heard the group before seeing them. There was no need for stealth as soon as he recognized the voices of his son and Tor. He shouted greetings to be sure there was no mistaken identity leading to a regrettable incident.

Ato and Tor did not talk about the trip right away. They would meet later in private after the explorers got some good food and rested. It would then be time for some important decisions for Ato as the chief and Tor as the high priest.

The next morning, Ato and Tor, accompanied by their eldest sons and Tor's nephew Lon, took a walk away from the village. It was not yet time to inform the villagers of the existence of others who were not quite like they were.

They lit a campfire in case day predators got curious and sat in a circle around it. Tor began. "The strange people hunted nearer to us this time, about this many sunrises travel from here, holding up both hands. The camps they abandoned also prove that they come often, and usually in the direction of our village.

Ato appeared worried and said, "Kor, when we get back to the village, select two men and send them out to find two more hills for us to send lookouts. We will then watch a larger area from which the strangers can approach. Select four young and fast warriors to take turns on the two new hills. Because you were a lookout for a long time, you are the best one to instruct them on what to do. You will attend all of the talks that Tor and I have from now on. If anything happens to me, you will be chief. Atu will replace Tor someday, and so he will also join us when we make plans. Lon, you will not be replacing anyone as of yet, but because of your experience with the outsiders, your words and thoughts will also be important."

Tor nodded and said, "Good plan, Chief. It will not be long before they get close enough to see or smell our fires, or run into one of our hunting parties. Lon has an idea that he wants to talk about and to ask for your approval. Lon, tell the chief your idea."

"Chief, it may be a good idea to learn more about these people. I would like to go back to where we met them and follow their trail all the way to their village. We can then spy on them to see how many there are and study them. Grandfather Og told us many stories, and many of them included important lessons. Among them, he mentioned that it is wise to know your enemies better than your friends."

Chief Ato looked at Tor and asked, "What do you think, Tor? Will the spirits approve?"

I believe it is a good idea, and I will consult with the spirits tonight. It may depend on whether their spirits are stronger than ours, or the same."

Ato said, "I will agree, depending on what your uncle tells me when the sun comes up. While you wait, choose some young warriors to travel with you. You know the young men better than I do. Pick those who are good hunters and are quiet. Loud ones may attract attention and create problems. I would say this many." Ato then held up four fingers. "Kor, help him select his party, and before you ask, no! You cannot go. A chief must lead, but not every day and in every way. When we finally meet these people, whether in battle or to talk, I will need you by my side."

Nito grunted to get attention and said, "Chief, Father, I would like to go with Lon. Although I am not yet a priest, they will need some spiritual guidance in such a long and dangerous journey. I learned to stalk from Lon too, and he knows what I can do."

"Tor," said Ato, "the brave young man may be my warrior, but he is also your son. I leave it to you to decide."

Tor nodded but allowed Lon to make the final decision because it was his responsibility to find the best men for the mission.

Og's widow, Su; Og's daughter Nia; Tor's wife, Tia; and Tor's daughter Lia got busy duplicating the spear thrower that Lon took from the strangers. The men made copies of the short spears that fit in the notch. In about a week, warriors practiced when not hunting or busy with village work. The younger tribe members, led by Lon and Kor, acquired proficiency faster than older warriors, who preferred the old way of throwing or thrusting spears from a shorter distance. During the next gathering of all the village priests, Tor told them to send ten young warriors from each village to train with the atlatl.

When the time came for testing their skill on moving targets, the men found that they could bring down bigger game. The short spears were longer and a little thicker than their flets, and therefore they were deadlier.

In earlier times, they occasionally hunted giant bears and mastodons but had to get closer. Their old spears were more effective in thrusting than throwing. The risk was too great, and so they concentrated on deer and smaller game. Now, with their combination of modern weapons, they did not need to get as close. The village's store of food, furs, bones and skins grew proportionately as their skills improved. The experiment with the smoke hut determined that smoke-treated meats remained edible longer than untreated meat.

Daily hunts were no longer essential. The tribe could take a day off now and then without fear of going hungry. The time saved proved valuable for rebuilding huts, searching for or excavating caves, and practicing with the arcs and atlatl.

CHAPTER 18

DISCOVERING PELU AND HIS TRIBE

Lon and Kor selected the four young men who would join Lon and Nito in the search for the strangers' home village. They took eight candidates on stalking forays and eliminated those who were less skilled and made too much noise while tracking.

The exploratory group included Lon as the leader; Nito; the older but crafty hunter and Mina's mentor Po; Oli, Ato's youngest; and Tau, Oli's cousin. The five loaded up with weapons, preserved meat, and thick furs on which to sleep.

They started out on a clear day facing the rising sun, which, as usual, gave them the direction to head for and enabled them to return. For the first week or so, they traveled with caution but not to excess. Thereafter, they moved more slowly and quietly, because they had no idea how far they needed to travel before reaching their goal.

The five made visual contact ten days later, a few miles farther west than Lon had seen them on his last journey. Now they moved with extreme care. They intended to follow them all the way back to their homes, not to confront them in the field. Lon recognized the leader as the same man he had seen before. Lon and Nito had a hard time keeping the other three men from overreacting to the unusual sight. Nito had heard all the stories and found it easier to remain calm.

Lon told them, "Look carefully. They are nearly the same as we are. They are taller and thinner, and they have less hair but dress nearly the same. None of us are identical. They are a little more different than we are from each other. For now, we are simply going to watch them. Listen to their words. Watch the one with the white and red stripes on his face; he is their leader. He must have a name. If you hear another call him, remember the sound. But do not get too close just to hear better; keep your distance. Only Nito and I will try to get closer when we feel it is safe. Remember, we must remain hidden until we find out where their village is. That may take a long time, so get used to it."

The outsiders prepared to make camp, and Lon knew that meant that it was safe to circle around them and take an observation position in the direction from which they had come. Po asked, "How do you know they won't come back the other way?"

"Because they are building a smoke hut and preparing the site for the night fire. They will not hunt in the direction from which they came. That is the way home for them. For a few days, we will be safe from an unexpected meeting with them."

Lon and his party took a wide turn around the camp and looked for a safe place to keep watch. They discovered a low hill covered with trees and shrubbery, but with a good view of the strangers' campsite.

When settled, Lon took Nito aside. "Nephew, remind the men to ask Mu, the spirit of darkness, to protect them during the night, and to thank Alu for allowing the sun to rise."

"Uncle, why do we have to do this so far from the village for just three people?"

"Nito, the journey we are on now is an adventure—necessary and satisfying but only a temporary action. Spiritual teaching and control are life-long quests. We cannot allow doubt or suspicion to creep into the thoughts of even one person. Og, our grandfather, set us on a path designed to give us and our children comfortable lives while giving hope or some sense of purpose to all others. That is possible only by convincing others that my father, you, others in our family, and I are the only ones who speak for the spirits. Whatever we believe makes no difference, but all others must believe it. Do you understand now why we must never let our guard down and always show that we speak for the spirits, whether in the village or out in the wilderness?"

"Yes, I understand. I will gather them for a few minutes and lead them in their pleas and thanks."

"When you are done, assign them to guard duty. I will take the first turn."

The next morning, the strangers broke camp to begin their hunt. That gave the watchers a chance to gather some fruits and berries for breakfast and carefully explore the area. They had to make sure not to leave any sign that would expose them. They ventured east because they believed that the hunters would not go in that direction for at least several days.

The hunters returned and appeared upset with their lack of success. They'd only bagged a small deer, just enough to feed the party perhaps twice. Thanks to the loud exchange, Lon deduced that the leader's name was Pelu. He now had four words: *atlatl*, *cuvo*, *figo*, and the leader's name.

Lon heard three of the four words in one conversation, which he understood as "Pelu, cuvos [in] figo?"

The answer was a sharp "Li." Lon guessed it meant yes. His new vocabulary now consisted of five words.

The campers acted as if they were alone in the world. They kept their campfire going all night long, but no one stayed up as a sentry. Every hour or so, someone other than Pelu got up to add wood to the fire or to relieve himself. Lon's little group kept watch all night long. They had found a niche on the hill that was not really a cave but afforded protection from three sides. Although not required to stand guard, Lon would come out a few times during the night to keep whoever was watching company for a short while. His rationale, he told the guard on duty, was that he needed to commune with the spirits during the night when in possible danger.

The routine continued for several days. Finally, on the fourth afternoon, the hunters returned elated with the best catch of their expedition. They'd killed a giant cave bear and dragged it to their camp using a litter similar to the one used to carry off their smoked meats the last time. Lon had not tried to make one after seeing it before but was determined to instruct his tribe on its construction and use.

Some hunters began to skin and cut the beast into manageable chunks while others finished the smoke hut. Pelu issued orders to others, who got to work collecting some of the weapons and tying them to the litter. Lon realized that the group would leave in the morning, with the unarmed men pulling the loaded litter.

C H A P T E R 1 9

HEADING INTO
THE STORM

Lon called his men to the opposite side of their lookout hill to explain future strategy.

"Before the sun goes down, we make our way to the other side of their camp. They will march in this direction, and so we must get behind them. We do not need to be close on their tail. The litter they drag leaves a clear marker, which will be very easy to follow. I do not know how far we will travel. Stay alert for any fruit trees, berries, nuts, or even honey. We can quietly collect as much as we can carry, and that will provide food for us on the way. If we find a lot, we can make a small litter like theirs or baskets to carry even more. Now, let's head out before the night stalkers come looking for a meal."

The small band took another wide route around the hunters' camp and found a clearing where they could build a temporary shelter for the night. In the morning, they waited a while after sunup to resume their tracking. They warily approached the abandoned camp. Nito and Po circled the camp in opposite directions. When they met on the other side, they made sure the camp was empty before entering the clearing. The campfire was still hot, and they used it to cook some of the smoked meat they had brought with them. It might be their last chance to have a hot meal. Lon and the other men joined them, and after a hearty breakfast, they resumed their journey.

As expected, the trail was easy to follow, but they still maintained a stealthy pursuit. Every few miles, one of them climbed a high tree to scan the terrain ahead and catch a glimpse of their quarry.

During the second day on the trail, Lon saw a flock of birds flying low and frowned. Nito noticed and asked his uncle what was wrong.

"Grandfather Og once told me that low-flying birds meant a thunderstorm was coming."

"Why are you worried about a storm?

"If it is a heavy storm, it will wash away the trail."

"Oh. What can we do?"

"Get closer, and soon."

Nito relayed the order, and everyone moved on at a faster pace after climbing a tree to get a quick look and spot the oncoming clouds.

"Uncle, the skies are dark in the direction we are going. I saw no sign of the hunters. We may lose them even if we hurry."

"We still need to try. Let's go!"

The small party headed into the path of the storm, which was moving toward them, and they toward it. It was not a devastating event but was strong enough to wash away any spoor. They lost the trail, forcing them to hunker down to wait for the rains to pass. When it cleared, they set out again to locate the other group. Lon was sure Pelu's people would continue eastward and proceeded in that direction. The searchers spread out looking for any sign of passage. It took several hours, for them to finally pick up a fresh trail. Lon ordered a rest stop because it would soon be dusk, making it impossible to continue.

C H A P T E R   2 0
TONG'S TRIBE

The next morning, Lon sent Nito up a tree to spy on the pursued and gauge their distance. They resumed their march but with more caution. At midday, Lon heard the yells and sounds of a commotion ahead: screams of pain mingled with the yells. Lon recognized the sounds of battle. The strangers were fighting, but with whom?

Lon and his small group of men looked down into a shallow valley and saw Pelu and his men engaged with a larger party of similar-looking men. The only noticeable difference between the groups was that the second set of strangers wore body paint of different colors. Lon noted that only one wore the color red. The fact that he was the only one painted in that color, as well as his aggressiveness and commanding voice, left no doubt that he was in charge. Pelu's force was outnumbered. For every warrior he had, there were three attackers.

Nito asked Lon, "Are we going to help them?"

"No. Never join a fight that you cannot win. Our small group would not make a difference in the outcome. Better for Pelu to surrender or escape."

As if on cue, Pelu shouted what was obviously a signal to retreat. It was too late. His men caught spears or flets in their backs as they attempted to flee. A flet struck Pelu on his left thigh, but he yanked it out and continued to run. As the wounded warrior entered the brush, the red man yelled a command, and his men stopped the pursuit. They then turned around to the battleground and speared every man on the ground. Lon wondered why they tried to kill them twice, because some were obviously already dead. The remaining painted men gathered the spoils of the skirmish but did not use the litter. Each jubilant fighter grabbed a bundle and ran off to the south.

Lon decided to go after Pelu. He saw this as an opportunity he could not let pass. The wounded warrior was unarmed and presented no danger in his condition. They followed swiftly with no need for subterfuge. The angry roar of a giant cave bear brought the pursuers to an abrupt halt. Lon told his men, "He is in trouble. The bear will get him if we do not help."

They raced until they came upon a frightening sight. Pelu had scampered up a thin tree too small for the bear to climb but not large enough to withstand the beast's attempts to knock it down. Blood from Pelu's wound dripped down the bole of the tree, which the bear slurped up, adding a degree of frenzy to its efforts.

Lon took in the scene at a glance and rushed the bear, yelling his very own battle cry. Lon's blood ran cold when he saw the wooly animal turn to look at him. With an unnerving roar of its own, it charged. On the run, Lon notched his short spear and let it fly. The spear made good contact, but it was as disabling as a mosquito bite in a man's buttocks. As Lon prepared to continue what now appeared to be a futile engagement, Po appeared from the left side of the creature, leaped high in the air, and buried his long spear far into its left shoulder, deep enough to pierce the heart. The behemoth stood on his rear legs and fell backward, nearly crushing Po, who was still trying to get up.

Lon pulled his short spear from the still creature and plunged it through its exposed throat. He smiled when remembering what he'd thought while the painted men tried to re-kill Pelu's already dead warriors. In this case, though, an animal this huge could take a man's head off with just a death spasm. It was better to make sure.

He left the embedded spear and walked toward the bewildered man still in the tree. Lon said only one word, "Pelu," understanding that most people react to their names before most other sounds. Pelu was puzzled but realized he was no longer in danger, and he painfully yet gratefully climbed down from his perch.

Lon tapped his chest and spoke his name. He then pointed to the injured man and said his name. Pelu understood even though he wondered how this savage knew his name. Lon had Nito gather small medicinal leaves to stuff the wound and some bigger ones to use as a bandage. When Nito gave him the plants, Lon raised them to the sun and mumbled gibberish. Nito smiled to himself but showed no evidence that he was aware of his uncle's intention. Lon planted the seed of his spiritual authority in Pelu's mind. Lon rinsed the wound with water, stuffed the puncture with the crushed small leaves, and covered it with the large leaves. He then tied the dressing in place with thin vines.

Communication between the hominids was difficult but not impossible. Naming physical items was easy: picking up or pointing at a rock, leaf, or other item with each man stating the name in their corresponding language. Lon's people called a bear *os*; Pelu's clan named it *ur*. Abstract words were more difficult to determine. While Pelu recovered, the two men used gestures and pantomime to learn enough in a few days to deliver simple messages. Nito paid close attention and learned along with his uncle. The rest of the crew showed little interest but stayed busy skinning their kill and smoking the meat. They ate well for the first time in a moon's cycle.

Po, Oli, and Tau took time to visit the scene of the painted men's attack. They buried the dead in shallow graves, gathered the scattered weapons, packed them in the litter, and dragged them back to their current camp.

CHAPTER 21
PELU'S VILLAGE

When Pelu was strong enough to travel, Lon asked him where he lived. He pointed to Pelu and then to different directions, mimicking a walk. Pelu understood immediately and indicated east. Lon had the men hide their cache of collected weapons to recover on their return trip. They then set out to find Pelu's home. The journey took half a moon's cycle. While en route, the two leaders and Nito learned enough of each other's language to carry on more complex conversations.

A subject came up that was extremely difficult for Lon to explain and even more so for Pelu to understand. Pelu was curious about the ritual with the plants used to dress his wounds. Lon did his best with the limited foreign vocabulary at his command. How does one describe an unseen, unknowable, ethereal being using gestures and pantomime? Lon believed that he got part of the message through when Pelu pointed to the sun and then the sky, touched the trees, knelt to caress the ground, and swept his arms in an all-encompassing gesture. Lon nodded approvingly. During times of rest, Lon drew the spirits symbols on the ground with a stick. He named each one, went to his knees, and reached to the sky with open arms. Pelu appeared puzzled, and Lon ended the lesson there.

Later, Nito asked, "How did the lesson go?"

"I don't know, but the seed is planted. Now we need to water and nurture it daily."

Some subjects were easier to discuss. Nito wanted to know about the painted men. Pelu said they came from the north. They had lighter skin and blond hair, and they showed no mercy in battle. They sought to kill and steal all they could. Interrogated prisoners said that the tribe was migrating to escape the colder weather that was creeping south. There was little vegetation, and therefore less game, a few moons' march to the north.

"Where did your people come from?" asked Nol.

"We are from the south. It has taken many moons to get this far. I was just a boy when we started. My grandfather was the chief; now my father leads the tribe."

"How will we be received? We are a bit different."

"I don't know, Lon. I am the chief's son, not the chief—unless he died in my absence. My people have been wary since the painted men came from the north. But do not worry; I will protect you. It may be best for me to go into the village first and tell my father the whole story."

"Just in case, send a signal so we can make our escape if they are not very welcoming."

Both men laughed and continued in halting but pleasant conversation.

Lon and his men were amazed when they saw Pelu's village. They had no caves. Some huts were made of straw, but some were made out of logs, and yet others were of animal skins. There were many smoking huts and many more cooking fires. The compound was much larger than their own. That indicated the tribe itself numbered many times more than their tribe. A force that large could overwhelm theirs in a very short time. Lon told Nito that those facts gave him pause to nurture any relationship between the two tribes.

Pelu entered the village to a huge welcome. Chief Teru led the welcome party but was anxious to get details of his son's travels. They retired to the largest structure in the village, made of logs, mud, and a thatched roof. Animal furs, skins, and tusks adorned the interior. Earthenware on shelves and weapon displays on the walls added to the décor. The collection of possessions also heralded the extent of their wealth and power.

The two sat on mounds of pelts and waited for Pelu's mother to bring in their meal.

"Tong attacked again. They killed my whole hunting party and stole everything we had."

"Then how is it that you are here?"

"I ordered a retreat when I saw that we could not win. The few left after the surprise attack caught spears in their backs as we ran. I was wounded too, but Tong called his men back when I entered the woods. He must have assumed I would die from the wound anyway. They then gathered the meat and ran off."

"How is it you did not die of the wound?"

"That is the strangest part of the story. Savages from a faraway village saved me."

"Savages? What savages, and why would they help you?"

"I call them that because of how they look, not how they behave. At first, I saw them as ugly and brutish, but they turned out to be intelligent, incredibly fearless, and excellent hunters. Just two of them brought down a giant cave bear that was trying to get me out of a tree. Their leader healed my injury and fed me while I recovered."

"What happened to them?"

"They escorted me home and are waiting outside the village."

"You brought them here?"

"What's the difference, Father? The Nors are our real enemies and they know where we are. They know better than to attack us here. In fact, I made sure Lon, their leader, understood that our village is secure. He did give me some advice that I would like to share with you. He said, 'If a mosquito bothers you, do you not swat it?'"

"What does that mean?"

"It means that we allow Tong to run wild, raiding our hunting parties and killing our men, and we do nothing about it."

"What does your savage mentor suggest?"

"Simple: go after him and eliminate the threat once and for all."

"Son, I would like to meet this… savage."

Soon after, Teru, Pelu, and three others escorted Lon and his men into the village. Many villagers came out to see the strange sight. Fortunately for Tor and his men, their limited understanding of the language kept them from grasping the full meaning of the insults and taunts. The visitors entered the chief's hut and accepted food and drink. The chief noticed how comfortable his son was conversing with the savage leader even though they spoke haltingly using both languages, switching back and forth as needed.

The chief had no idea where the conversation was going, let alone what they were saying. Pelu translated. "Lon said that we should send a hunting party to the area where Tong has attacked most often. After the hunters leave, send reinforcements to trail them. He believes that they watch our village. The spy sees when the hunters go out and rushes to warn the Nors, who then ambush them after they have made some kills."

"How does he know this?"

"First, common sense. He is not only a shaman but a strategist in his village."

"A shaman?"

"Yes. He talks to the spirits and asks for good weather, success in hunts or battles, and other natural events. His people believe that invisible beings control everything that affects people and the world."

"I have heard about invisible beings that control the world for years, since I was a boy, and that there must be some explanation for rain, the moon, and the stars. Why they come and go and why we must suffer at times. But I've never received an explanation or answers to my questions. The most I got was, it's just the way it is."

"Yes, Father. That is what he tries to explain – why and how things happen, and the spirits responsible for events that affect us all. He does not expect the storms to stop suddenly, or that there will only be pleasant days forever. But he tries to lessen the effects and gives his people strength to cope with the bad times and enjoy the good ones. He also tries to give them advice. He warns them not to depend on the spirits to take care of all their problems. If they are hungry, he tells them to find some fruit or catch a rabbit. The gods are not going to serve you a meal through magic. The spirit guide's obligation is to lead the people in thanking the gods and honoring them in order to keep them happy so that they provide better weather and good hunts, and keep them safer. The obedient servants or believers may maintain better lives. The beliefs also make it easier to explain when things are not going so well."

"Better that they have someone else to complain to than me, or you when you are chief. Tell him I like him, and he is welcome in our village any time."

"I think he already knows that, because he understands our language better than I do his."

Lon spoke directly to the chief for the first time. "Thank you, Chief Teru. I appreciate your invitation. I will speak to my chief, and I am sure that your people will be welcome in our village too. When our people learn your language, I may send one to introduce you to our gods, and maybe you will see how knowing and understanding them will make for better lives."

"Look around at my home and our village. I believe that we are doing quite well as we are, without the interference of unseen creatures."

Lon chose his response carefully. "Yes, Chief Teru. May your fortunes continue to grow, and may the spirits guide you in eliminating the annoyance of Tong and his thievery. I sought guidance after learning of Tong and his evil acts. My spirit of war, Ra, presented a vision of the painted men on the run chased by your brave warriors."

"Does that vision foretell what is to come?"

"No, Chief, but it's one of the possible outcomes if Ra is pleased with the steps your people take."

"So, if Tong's people take the right steps, your Ra may side with him and his desires?"

"Many moons ago, before I was born, my grandfather Og was chosen to receive spiritual insight. He began the doctrines we now follow. Your tribe is the first outside our own to receive the word of Og. It is not possible for Tong or his people to have made similar discoveries. Your tribe has done very well, so I must assume that you and your people have pleased the gods with your activities or behavior. I'm simply imagining how much better off your great clan would be if you acknowledged the gifts of the spirits."

"Lon, your words are interesting. It would have been an honor to have met your grandfather and exchanged stories. I hear from Pelu that he lived for very many seasons and was very wise. I would like to learn more of these gods. I don't see how it can hurt."

"We are grateful for welcoming us and for your kind words. I hope you will someday meet my father, Tor. He can tell you more about my grandfather and understands the spirits and their ways much better than I do."

CHAPTER 22

AMBASSADOR EXCHANGE

Lon and his band spent a restful night in Pelu's beautiful settlement. In the morning, Lon proposed an idea to Nito. "Nito, if Pelu's father agrees, would you care to stay here for a few moons to learn the language thoroughly and introduce them to our spirits? I believe they have thought about the unexplained mysteries of nature. Perhaps you can enlighten them, or at least steer them in that direction."

"Yes, I can stay. But don't you mean in *our* direction?"

"Hmm, you're right. Let me speak with Pelu and see whether he likes the idea. Be careful and do not be too pushy. Go slow, let the words simmer, and add more only after the previous words are absorbed or digested. This is a lifetime duty. There is no need to explain everything in one sitting. Keep them longing for more. The more questions they ask, the more their interest grows."

Lon presented the idea to Pelu, who agreed but added a condition. "Take one of our young men with you. Teach him your language and let him experience how your people live. It will be a fair exchange."

"That would be great. Talk to your father. If he agrees, my band can head home with the lucky young man you select."

A short time later, Pelu met again with Lon and presented Neru, his younger brother, as the fortunate young man selected to experience the adventure of a lifetime. Lon was impressed with the boy, who displayed confidence and a genuine interest in travelling. The journey would provide learning and bonding opportunities for both Lon and Neru.

It was time to return home. Lon asked for and received a large, well-armed escort to accompany them until they were one full day away from the village. When on their own, they left several false trails to confuse any followers. Lon told the men that he trusted Pelu but was not so sure about the chief or other members of the tribe. During the long hike back, Lon spent every waking moment instructing Neru and adding more words to his own foreign vocabulary. He found Neru to be very intelligent and eager to learn. During the trip, they developed a close relationship that Lon hoped would be beneficial to both their tribes in the future.

Lon learned that Neru's people called themselves Croms, and that many moons ago, they had come from the south as explorers. They did not leave because of great hardship, but to see what else was out there. His grandfather had shown him drawings of many strange animals that did not exist in this area. He said that someday he would like to go back to his people's lands of origin. Lon said, "If it continues to get colder, we may all have to go."

In addition to teaching the boy a new language, Lon also sprinkled in spiritual notions to begin his indoctrination into the world of gods and lesser ethereal beings. Neru appeared skeptical at first, but out of respect for the older man, he listened carefully, asked questions, and gradually gained acceptance. By the time they arrived at Lon's village, Neru was almost an acolyte.

The journey itself was not extraordinary, but it was instructive. Both Lon and Neru gained proficiency in their respective languages and each other's cultures. Neru benefited from stalking and hunting lessons from Po and Lon. The older men learned about fishing, which they seldom if ever practiced. The Croms usually built settlements near rivers or lakes and depended on seafood, though not as much as the game found in the forest. They also grew edible crops, including tubers.

Lon was slightly disappointed that the group did not encounter any giant bears or longtooths—not out of a desire to face greater danger, but (perhaps perversely) to test Neru's courage or to display his own. Although they traveled leisurely, they made good time because they did not encounter any adverse conditions of weather or other dangerous situations.

As in the past, the lookouts emplaced in the hills around their village perimeter saw their approach as they neared the village. A welcoming reception of ten villagers, this time led by Ato and Tor, met the expedition near the edge of the settlement. Neru attracted the focus of attention. He stayed near Lon, where he felt safer in the midst of all these strange people. Lon's first move was to pull Tor and Ato aside for a brief time to inform them that the boy understood their language, and to wait until they were alone before asking questions and reacting to or divulging private information.

Tor's first question concerned the whereabouts of his son Nito. Lon responded, "We sort of traded him for the Crom leader's younger son."

"What? You traded my boy for a stranger?"

"No, Uncle, not quite like that. He chose to stay for a few moons to learn all he could about their language, culture, and even their long-term plans. Neru is here for the same reason. Two high-ranking tribal members living in each other's company may help make the relationship successful."

"Could he be in any danger?"

"I don't believe so. He is the personal guest of Pelu, the chief's son and the man Po and I saved from the jaws of a giant bear. He and I became close friends soon after that incident. Nito is also the only one beside me who could impress them with our spiritual values and lead them in that path."

Tor smiled inwardly, understanding his nephew's true intent, but he did not question it further in the company of others. They had much to talk about in private.

C H A P T E R   2 3
STRANGERS IN FOREIGN LANDS

On entering the village itself, Neru drew even closer to Lon when surrounded by most of the village dwellers, who were more than curious about the strange visitor. Tor glanced at Ato, who understood the silent message. Ato ordered the gawkers and pawers to stand back or return to their duties. The crowd dispersed, easing the growing concern troubling the young visitor.

Tor addressed the nervous boy. "Neru, stay close to Lon for now. Soon the people will get used to you, and it will be as if you have always been part of their lives. I am sure that my son Nito is experiencing the same concerns as you. Relax, and you will be fine. But if you have any difficulty with anyone, tell Lon, Chief Ato, Po, or me. Better still, get to know my daughter Mina. Do not be fooled by her age or size. You can be sure that while with her, not even the toughest man in the village will dare even look at you threateningly."

"I understand. I too have to get used to the changes in my life and accept your people as I do my own. Mina is the one who took down a saber tooth, right?"

"Yes. Come to my cave after you get some rest. You can meet her there; also, my mother and mate have some gifts for you."

Despite the ease of their return trip, the party was still tired and slept through the rest of the day until the next morning. On rising, they all went to Tor's cave, where Su and Nia gave Neru a leather necklace adorned with gold icons of Alu, the spirit leader, and Ka, the hunter spirit. The grateful boy beamed with pleasure, saying he would never take it off. He also met Mina and both agreed to spend some time together so that she could learn his language and in turn, he would learn from her.

Lon said, "You two never made one for me."

Nia answered, "You never brought anything to trade."

"He did not bring anything either."

"Yes, he did," Su said. "He brings mystery, surprise, and a smile."

Tor enjoyed the sarcastic but friendly exchange, but he needed to get down to serious business with his nephew. They charged Po with escorting Neru around the village while uncle and nephew took a stroll in the woods to answer questions and question answers.

"Now, Lon, tell me what happened. Not necessarily from the beginning, but from the moment you came across Pelu and his band."

"We found them about ten days closer to our village than when we first discovered them, which meant that they were foraging farther from their base. I did much the same as we did on our foray, so there is nothing new there. We lost the trail due to a storm but found it again. The first big difference was their battle with the painted men. They are the people about whom we must worry. They are fearless, brutal, and relentless, and they take no prisoners. There was no choice except to watch the carnage. We acted only to chase the wounded Pelu after the killers disregarded his escape.

"Perhaps the most exciting event was watching Po strike the deathblow on the bear. Mere words cannot describe his leap behind the beast and his uncanny aim. One had to be there to fully appreciate his skill and bravery. That thing would have killed us all had he not been there. All of us there will be forever grateful for what he did. Although I struck the first blow, I let Po have the head and fur as trophies."

Lon remained quiet for a few moments, still enthralled by that one thrilling minute that would forever define his lust for adventure and his love of life.

Tor nudged him out of his mesmerized stupor with a loud, "Hey!"

"Oh, sorry. I could not help but relive that episode. It seems to haunt me even when awake. Let me continue. We then settled into an uneventful trek to his village. We were concerned that the red man and his savages might find us, but we took extra precaution by climbing trees every so often to scan ahead and avoid surprise.

"I hope that someday you will see their village. Our village would fit inside it many times. There are so many people that they could destroy us in one full-strength attack. That is one reason why Nito and I decided to nourish our friendship. It's better to have them as allies than enemies. We also may need their help if the painted ones ever find our village.

"Nito is also trying to introduce them to our spiritual beliefs. We need more in common than simply having the same number of legs and arms. Uncle, there are other things that worry me. They are more advanced than we are. Their huts are not flimsy straw huts but are solid, made out of wood and baked mud. There were crews building walls in vulnerable areas, and armed men on perches watching all the time. They will not suffer surprise raids. The average tribal member appears to be more intelligent than our people."

"What did you say?"

"Please do not get angry, Uncle. You know that you, my mother, other members of our close family, and I are different than others in our tribe. It must be because of Grandfather Og. He was healthier, older, and wiser than anyone our people have ever seen. He also began teaching you and Nia from the time you could barely walk. You did the same for Atu and Nito, and Mother began my lessons early too. It may not be that we are smarter than the others, but that we got a head start. It is possible that because of the early lessons, we think and solve problems faster."

"You know, Lon, Og suspected the same. He always knew that he was unusual, although he never let the others think that he was different. At least, not until he got too old to hunt and invented the spirits out of desperation and the desire to survive. He did not have children with his first two mates; otherwise, his situation might have changed earlier."

"That change in life situations may have been very interesting for the old man, but had he had children when younger with either of his earlier mates, we would not be here now."

"Lon, I never thought of that. I guess that makes us very lucky, or maybe the gods planned it that way."

"Maybe, but is that something Grandfather would want us to believe?"

"No, Lon, he would not. And none of us believe that either, but it will make a good subject to explore in the future. Now, I have to talk to Ato."

Tor met with Ato to explain the danger of the painted men and to help make plans should they discover the village. The hilltop guards received detailed instructions and were told to be especially watchful for men who looked like Neru but had painted bodies and lighter hair.

Within a full moon's time, Neru felt comfortable enough to wander about the village without a protector. He was also sufficiently confident to join the hunting parties, and more important, he developed a friendship with Tor's daughter, Lia. The differences in appearance no longer mattered to Neru and the people of the village. He still found time to spend with Mina as she was eager to gain proficiency in the new language. The most interesting and somewhat comical part of walking around with the young girl was how others stepped aside when she approached. It seemed to be out of respect and awe, not fear.

In the faraway village of the Crom, Nito also became more active in the foreign village. His wanderings around the camp no longer drew strange looks. He was now no more interesting than any other villager. However, he was hypersensitive to his surroundings and absorbed every bit of information that came to his ears and eyes. Even his sense of smell remained very active, savoring the aromas of foreign foods to which he became accustomed. Pelu had suggested that other siblings attend to Nito when he was drawn to other village activities. Nito's favored escort was Fela, Pelu's younger sister. The two became good friends as they spent more time together and understood each other better.

From a distance, Pelu's village was under observation daily. The spies wondered about the strange visitor in the village and informed Tong. Pelu's hunting parties were now larger in number, and attacking them was no longer wise. The village itself was impossible to raid due to the greater number of warriors and the precautions taken to avoid surprise.

Tong and his band had no choice but to hunt for their own game and hope for the infrequent small parties that came across their path.

CHAPTER 24
NITO'S RETURN

When the moon completed three cycles, Nito told Pelu that it was time for him to go back home, and to send back Neru. Pelu arranged for a large force to make the journey to ensure a safe return for both ambassadors.

On the day of departure, Tong's spies noted the exaggerated activity and sent a runner to relay the news. Tong came to investigate himself and determined that this was no typical hunting party. It looked like they planned to travel far. He assumed that it might be to take the odd-looking outsider to where he had come from. Tong studied the scenario and considered possible actions. The group was too large to attack and carried nothing of value. He chose to follow. Tong picked his three best trackers, and he would lead them in following the group. He told his remaining troops to stop observing the village and build a more permanent camp to await his return. "No raids while I'm gone," he told them. "Hunt for your own needs. I do not know how far we will travel, and I have no way of knowing how long we will be. Just wait."

There was no way for such a large troop of people to travel and not leave a clear track. Tong's band had no need stay close or worry about losing the trail. There was no risk of discovery.

The assembly of Croms was fearless due to their number, and they made no attempt at subterfuge and proceeded with minimum caution. They hunted and gathered along the way. There was no shortage of nourishment, making their trek pleasant if not swift. They still made good time, and in nearly a moon, they neared Nito's territory.

The watchers on the hill spied the large party from far away and ran down to alert Ato. The chief gathered a large number of warriors. Joined by Tor, he set out to meet the approaching group. Tor suspected it was Neru's people and took him along. In short intervals, Neru climbed trees to get a better look. After the third climb, he said excitedly, "Tor, it's my brother Pelu and your nephew Nito." Tor knew of a small clearing along their route and chose to wait there to avoid suddenly startling the approaching throng in the thick woods. The two most recognizable, Neru and Po, would be the most apparent to the visitors. Pelu and Nito also came to the same conclusion as they marched in front of their own groups.

From a treetop not very far away, the most attentive eyes belonged to Tong. He watched with great interest as he took in the odd sight of two very different tribes meeting as if they were long lost friends. Tong was puzzled but intrigued. Now the tracking had to continue, but with more stealth and cunning. He scanned the area in the direction the two united parties went and was not surprised to notice lookouts on three hills. He considered sneaking up on the hill guards and killing them, but that might not be wise at this time. He ordered his men to familiarize themselves with the terrain and the positions of the posted observers. That information would be important when they returned with the entire army.

They circled the hills, remaining wary of any other guard posts. It seemed that they expected an approach from only one direction. *How fortunate,* he thought. The noise from the village alerted the stalkers to its location. They found a secure niche hidden from their opponent's view, and they settled in to survey defensive positions. They counted the men, looked for weapon caches, and assessed fortifications and guard posts. The huts were thatched and easily put to fire. The cave dwellings were another matter; a strategy to attack them was essential.

As the enemy watched and schemed, the reunited families exchanged greetings and delivered news. Tor, Pelu, Ato, Nito, and Neru stepped away from the commotion in the village center to discuss future relations for both tribes. They were too far apart to engage in any form of trade or barter, but they did expect to maintain contact in some form. Pelu said, "I believe that Nito may want to go back with us. He and my sister are … close friends."

"Interesting," said Tor. "Your brother Neru has become attached to my daughter Lia."

The embarrassed boys glanced at each other and could do little more than smile and blush. The blush was less apparent on the hairier Nito.

Tor and Pelu were intrigued but not surprised that the two boys chatted away expertly in either language without stumbling for words or noticeable hesitations. It was a good sign that mutual benefits were a distinct possibility. The two leaders understood that the first step in any alliance was communication. Obviously, conversation enhanced cooperation and interrelations. Any fears that previously apparent differences could be impediments to coexistence were easily dispelled after witnessing the almost instant connection between the two young men.

Pelu and his people stayed for a week to recuperate from the long journey, and to gather supplies for the return trip. The only contentious issue revolved around the two boy ambassadors, Nito and Neru. Nito was older, almost a man, and it was time for him to form a family. The decision for him to leave his people and reunite with Fela was easier. Neru was younger and missed his Crom family, but he also did not want to be apart from Lia. Tor began to wonder whether he had gained a son or lost a daughter. The answer was obvious: his daughter chose to go with Neru.

Tong noticed that the Crom planned their return, and he decided that it was best to leave a day or so ahead so as not to need caution following. He and his three men could make faster time by following the trail left by the large group, with no concerns over leaving signs because their outgoing tracks would mingle with the incoming ones.

CHAPTER 25
SIGNS OF DANGER

The large group left with the morning sun. Pelu now had a new sister and a very happy little brother. He ordered his warriors to protect her at all costs.

Several days on the road found Nito and Neru chatting and leading the march. They were many paces ahead of the trailing company when Nito stopped suddenly. His sharp eyes and skill as a tracker noticed something odd in the path they followed. Footsteps in the opposite direction were not the only clue. "Neru, run back and get Pelu—quick!" said Nito.

Neru's excitement incited Pelu to greater speed. On his arrival, Nito shared his findings, "See? Fresh footsteps going east. Look at the leaves: yellow markings on them and brushed in the same direction. The painted men were here and went this way."

"You are right. We may have made a big mistake not watching our backs. They followed us to your village and now are hurrying back to their own camp."

"Looks that way," said Nito. "It appears that it was a very small party no more than the fingers in one hand, unless the larger trail has obscured the passing of others."

"They can travel much faster than we can. We cannot catch them, but we must hurry anyway. I will send two men back to your village to warn Ato and Tor. It will be very difficult, but we must come back with many men to defend your people."

"No, just one man has to go now. I cannot abandon my people. Tell Fela that I am sorry but will return to her later."

With those words, Nito took off, accompanied by one of Pelu's warriors at his insistence. They took very short rests and got back in half the time it took them to reach the point of discovery.

Chief Ato, Tor, Lon, and Nito discussed several strategies for defense. It would take the returning painted men at least a full moon to get back to where they came from. They could make it to the village in perhaps a moon and a half, depending on the size of their force.

Ato asked, "How did they get past our hill watchers?"

Tor said, "They were following Pelu's unit, so to avoid discovery, they probably kept track from another hill or treetop and saw the posts from a distance. Once their positions were known, it was easy to simply avoid them."

For many days, village activity was virtually nonstop. Women, children, and older men fashioned arcs, flets, short, and long spears. Night guards were doubled, and fires were kept lit all night long. Hunting parties increased in number. More food was stored in case of a drawn-out war. Neighboring villages followed suit in preparation. Runners took positions on platforms high in trees. If one village came under attack, the nearest runner was to head to an adjoining village to get help.

Nito assured Ato that Pelu would return with his own warriors to lend assistance. Ato asked, "Won't his village be in danger of attack?"

"Maybe," said Nito. "But their village is very strong, and they have many warriors. Also, Tong and his force will be coming here first."

CHAPTER 26
SAVING THE FAMILY

Ato's village was ready, but the chief did not truly appreciate Tong's cunning and skill in tactical warfare. Tor had pleaded for long-range patrols of several men in various directions to further avoid surprises. Ato refused, saying every man was needed in the village. "Besides," Ato said to Tor, "you can talk to the spirits. Ask them to keep us safe."

Tor walked away, slightly shaking his head and wondering whether he had created a monster by making his people believe that the nonexistent gods born of Og's imagination would magically deign to help them in battle.

The believers failed to accept the lesson that pleas alone meant nothing. One must act. Asking for a good hunt did not replace actually going out to hunt. He gathered his family and gave them a set of instructions. Should Tong and his brutal men attack, and it appeared that stopping them was impossible, the family members were to try to escape. An attempted escape was better than a sure death.

"Where do we go?" asked his wife, Tia.

"You all know where we took Og in his last days. That is arid land, where there is no water or game. No hunter or warrior would go there. That is where we will meet. Take only a weapon, a pouch of water, and food for at least a few days. Wait no more than two days. After that, you can be sure that anybody not there will be dead, including me. After the second day, make your way east and look for the Crom village. That is the best we can hope for. Some of you do not know the land I refer to, but Nia does, and she can guide you."

The younger nephews and grandsons, not yet men, protested. "But, Tor, we are warriors too and want to do our part."

"I know, and you do have a job. Your part is to protect your siblings and your mothers, and to ensure your future. That is a big enough job for any warrior. It is not a sure thing that escape is necessary. If the battle does not go well, I will give a signal for you to leave. If we are winning, there is no need for signals."

Mina spoke up too, "Why was I and other females allowed to learn to use arcs and flets if we cannot join the battle?"

Tor said, I have relieved you from hill duty for a specific reason. Atu will lead the escape if necessary but may not be able to fight adequately with only one good arm. Your extraordinary skills are essential to stand beside him and help protect our people as they flee the doomed village. The ones engaged fighting the main attack may not be able to cover the family's backs."

Nia said, "Father, suppose the battle is not going well but you cannot give the signal."

"Good point! Atu, I want you to stay near this cave. If I cannot signal, you must make the decision. A good leader also needs to know when to disengage. Mina, you will essentially be Atu's weapons. Your job is to cover his back as he concentrates on leading the family to safety. There is no one I would trust more to do this than you."

Mina said, "Thank you father, I will not let you down.

Atu agreed with the plan and the whole family began preparing what they would need if escape became the only option.

Atu, Nito, Lon, and Tor met frequently during the next few days. They wanted to examine all the possibilities they could think of. Tor spoke first to his oldest son. "Atu, you would have great difficulty fighting vicious warriors with only one good arm. You are the oldest son and have been practicing priesthood longer than Nito. Your job is to preserve our legacy and beliefs. Pass them on to our young ones and whoever may cross your path in the future. I already gave you instructions to escape to Og's mountain if the invasion is successful.

"Nito, I know you are brave, but that should not lead to foolishness. When I was young, Og allowed me to go into battle but advised me to stay near Ato and his best warriors. I want you to be alongside Po, who is even better than Ato. If the war does not look good for us, leave. Join the rest of the family in their hideout. It would be best if one or both of you led the family to a better place and safer life. I will do my best to be with you, but in this situation, I am a better warrior than a priest. My pleas to the gods will not harm a single enemy, but my flets and spear will. When the fighting starts, you two make your way to the vicinity of my cave. The family will move there at first sign of attack. If they must leave, cover their departure until you can also get away. Remember, your primary duty is to protect yourself, then your family, and then the tribe. Your loyalty belongs to the smallest group you associate with or call your own. Prepare an emergency escape packet with a weapon, food, and water, and store it somewhere along the path to Father's final resting place. I will be with Ato and Kor for the rest of the day. May the gods favor you." All of them laughed at the hollow blessing and moved on to take care of their duties.

Tor found Ato and Kor in a sour mood. They were afraid, and rightfully so. It was Tor's job to bolster their spirits and give them some comfort and hope. He felt pretty much the same but had mastered the art of concealing feelings and emotions. A speaker for the gods could not show fear.

"Ato, Kor, be still. Worrying now does no good. Too many people spend time worrying about what might happen. If the feared event does not occur, all that time was wasted. If it actually happens, the act of worrying did nothing to prevent it. So why be concerned about what might be? It's better to plan for various possibilities. 'If this happens, I do that. If that happens, I do this.' It is more productive than wasting time lamenting, worrying, or complaining.

"There is no doubt the enemy is coming. What we do now determines whether our people survive or perish. It is my duty to advise you, Chief Ato, but you must make the hard decisions. Kor, it is up to you to add counsel. First, what do we know? The painted men are coming, and they are efficient killers. They do not show mercy; they will kill us all and take what they want. Second, what do we do? We have lookout posts. I suggest we increase them. A party of men should stay awake all night inside the village, prepared to fight. Put our best archers on perches in trees to fire flets down at the enemy."

"Wait!" shouted the chief. "I believe we are ready to defend the village as we always have. We also have the help of the spirits you talk to all the time."

"Gods have no interest in what to them are petty squabbles among people. They care only about controlling nature, the sacrifices we offer, and receiving worship. All a priest can do is keep them from getting too angry and destroying us all. In a war, they do not care who dies. They will favor the victors."

"Kor and I will consider your suggestions later. We are joining the hunt today."

Disappointed, Tor walked away to make plans of his own to save as many as possible.

CHAPTER 27
THE MARCH TO WAR

Tong and his small party made excellent time. The red leader had schemed and plotted during their journey, and he began implementing the plans immediately after arriving at the temporary camp. The first step was to send runners to his tribe's permanent encampment and return with more warriors. He then sent hunting parties to build up a supply of food to sustain them during their coming crusade. He wanted to minimize the need to hunt during that time.

Pelu's assemblage also hurried, but due to their numbers, they could not travel as fast. On arrival at their village, he explained the situation to his father, but Teru did not share his sense of urgency. It took Pelu several days of near disrespectful pleading to convince the Crom leader that Nito's people needed help. The convincing argument may have been the reminder that Lon had saved his life. Pelu suspected that it was Lia's appearance and Neru's attachment to her that troubled his father.

Tong's army moved out two days before Pelu's assemblage—very bad timing for Lia's home village. They marched west carrying only weapons and just enough food and water for an expeditious, one-way journey. There was little need to gather more along the way because they expected to load up to maximum capacity for their return home with the bounty from the sacked village.

Pelu went in the same direction with an equal sized force. They also traveled with due haste, but the enemy had a head start and moved faster.

Half a day's march from Ato's village, Tong stopped and sent six silent assassins to dispatch the three hill guards and any others posted around the perimeter when they arrived at their posts. The remainder of the attackers could then approach undetected at sunup.

The three young men scheduled for hill duty rose as usual just before sunrise. They ate a simple breakfast and made their way to their assigned hill post. Almost simultaneously, Tong's executioners sliced the watchers' throats as they arrived at the base of their respective hills. The same fate befell the three unfortunate villagers assigned to patrol the outskirts.

Rested, Tong's multicolored band moved out before the sun rose. They planned to commence their attack just as the sun peeked over the horizon.

CHAPTER 28
VILLAGE ASSAULT

At the appointed hour, Tong's men entered the village, set on killing as many as possible before their targets were fully awake. Fortunately for some tribal members, the dogs they had become accustomed to, raised an alarm of unceasing barks. Screams mingled with war cries aroused the rest of the sleeping warriors, and the battle raged. Tong and his men had planned to set the grass huts full of sleepers on fire. They did not get the chance. Tor saw three men lighting torches in the campfires. He notched a flet and shot one fire starter. Another fell to his short spear, aided by an atlatl. He met the third in full charge and sent him to the afterlife with his long spear. Po joined him in the village clearing, and back to back, they dispatched any painted man who came near them.

"Po, find Nito," Tor yelled. "Fight beside him, but protect him. I will be fine."

No answer was necessary. Po moved quickly to find and protect his best friend's son. Tor continued fighting like a madman, firing flets when he had a second or two to notch one, and using the long spear other times. He even used the dropped torches when he discovered that the paint covering the savages' bodies burned easily.

More of his allies joined him in the center of the melee. He gave orders to target the red man, but Tong's personal escorts protected him well. The red leader had given a similar order aimed at Chief Ato. Tor noticed the increased assault on Ato and moved to help. He managed to let fly three flets in succession at the men rushing his chief and friend. The three targets dropped. Tor had no more missiles and watched in horror as Ato fell to a volley of blows and stabbings.

"Kor, come with me!" he yelled. Kor disengaged and ran to the battling priest's side. "You are chief now, Kor. We cannot win. Help from other villages may be on their way, but it will be too late. Better to save some of the people than lose them all. Give the order to abandon the village."

Kor did not protest. He yelled the order as loud as he could. Many fell during the retreat, but many more, if not all, would have died had they stayed.

Lon, bloodied but undaunted, appeared out of nowhere with a handful of flets and took a position between the attackers and his fleeing tribal members. He fired flets faster than any warrior on either side possibly could. As he downed the enemy one by one, he urged his people to get away. An enemy flet struck his left arm. It was a glancing blow but forced him to drop his arc and continue battling with the atlatl. He killed three more painted men before Tor arrived to help him. Without words and with a mere glance, they both realized the futility of continuing a battle that could only result in their deaths. They turned and ran out of the doomed village. The enemy did not pursue far; they had won, and it was time to collect their bounty. There was no sense in risking their own lives in an attempt to kill one or two more of the escapees.

Atu realized almost from the start, that the village was doomed. He ordered the family to head out as planned. Atu rushed ahead to direct the exodus and give support to his endangered family. Mina lingered behind to cover the fleeing family members. As Atu left, two of Tong's warriors approached them. Mina saw them coming and prepared to confront them. The men saw the girl standing defiantly in their way and started laughing. Their overconfidence and their inbred disrespect for females in their own tribe would lead to their downfall. The laughter stopped abruptly when her flet skewered one's throat. Mina had more flets and time to let one fly, but for some unknown reason chose a secondary weapon. Without much thought, she dropped her arc, picked up her battle-axe as her enemy took his first steps toward her. His final error was believing she planned to challenge him in hand-to-hand combat. Mina knew better, she had practiced long and hard for this moment; with both hands on the handle she reached back with the axe and let it fly. The business end of the axe split the shocked man's sternum in two. He dropped instantly. She was somewhat surprised and glad in a way, that killing men was far easier than killing tigers.

The now battle tested warrior-defender, followed her brother's trail while remaining wary of any of the invading horde's disengaged attackers. The young woman was proud of her actions and realized that she was destined to be a leader, not a follower. Someday, she knew, she would have her own tribe where women would play a much more important part in a village's affairs. For the moment, she put aside her dreams and concentrated on protecting her family's hasty departure.

The child Warrior hesitated, feeling incomplete. She was not born to retreat but to meet danger head on. No enemy warriors were chasing her family and her defense of them was no longer necessary.

Mina made a snap decision. She would pursue the invaders and although there was no way to engage them all in battle, she could pick off a few from a distance with well- placed flets. Mina's goal was a combination of selective revenge and to lessen their numbers in case they met again.

The victorious Tong and his marauders whooped in delight as the surviving villagers ran. It was surprising that the villagers were not chased and cut down on the run. The next few hours proved even more sadistic. All fallen villagers were impaled, even if already dead. Huts were burned, dogs were slaughtered, and caves were pillaged. They found treasures of gold and silver in what once was Tor's cave. It seems the painted men appreciated the shiny trinkets too. Tong ordered his lieutenants to pack everything of value: fur, skins, smoked meats, and other food. He wanted to leave the burning village as soon as possible. It was hot, and the stench of war and death would soon be unbearable.

There were many warriors and would leave a well-marked trail. There was no need for Mina to hurry. On the way she would pick up discarded flets, other weapons, water, and provisions to last a few days.

It only took a short time to pick up the attackers' spoor. At that point Mina switched from chasing in haste to pursuing with stealth. Mina had to travel as noiseless as the blink of an eye and select her targets with care. In any large group, there are leaders, followers and always, careless stragglers. The careless or slow would be the first on her list.

 She saw a lone painted man. He appeared fatigued. Her first flet provided eternal rest. As she let the missile fly, Mina blended into the forest. There was no need to follow the flight of her silent but deadly missile. She knew it would do its job.

The silent avenger continued her pursuit, taking down one enemy after another. After the first few she thought it better to go back and retrieve used arrows. At the rate she was going, her supply of arrows would be depleted quickly.

CHAPTER 29

SURVIVORS

Tor's family was long gone. Realizing there was no hope of prevailing, he had given the preordained signal as soon as the attack began, not knowing that Atu had already given the signal.

The fleeing warriors and villagers sensed they were out of danger and stopped a mile away at the river's edge. They washed their wounds, slaked their thirst, and rested. Tor and Lon arrived a short time later. Before conferring with Kor, Lon's injuries needed attention.

Tor said to Lon, "You are covered in blood. Wash it away in the river, and we can look after your injuries."

"The blood is not all mine, Uncle. I only have a slight gash on my arm from the last flet that hit me. The rest belonged to the enemy I slew with my ax and short spear. I am not sure if it helped, but I asked Ra for help while fighting. It almost made me really believe."

"It probably helped by giving you more energy. It did not occur to me to plead to the gods. I was hoping for Po to show up. His skill and spear are more useful than begging the invisible and non-existent for protection."

At that point, Kor approached and said, "What now, Tor?"

"You are the chief. What do you want to do? "

"I don't know. This is my first day as a chief, and I do not even have a village."

"You have people. With them, you can build a better village. The painted ones will not stay. They will take everything of value and return to their land. You cannot go back to our old village either; there are too many bodies to bury. It will be uninhabitable for a long time. This is one time where we must let nature take its course. Scavengers will do much of the cleaning. Storms and creeping vegetation will handle the rest in time. Is there a nearby village where you are usually welcomed and treated well?

"Yes. Ba is chief there, and one of your nephews, Tun, is beginning his priesthood."

"I know it well, and my nephew Tun is dependable. Send a runner with news of the battle and ask if the village survivors can stay for a while until you can build a new village. Always ask. Remember, you are not chief there. Do not stay long. Find an area you can settle as quickly as you can. Visitors are welcome, enjoyable, and bearable, but only for a short time."

"What will you do?"

"I sent word to Nito to leave right before I told you. I'm not sure if he got the message. I have to find my family. I will decide then which path I will follow."

Tor said his goodbyes. He sensed that he had seen Kor and what was left of his tribe for the very last time.

He and Lon moved quickly in the direction of Og's mountain, where he hoped his family waited.

CHAPTER 30
MINA'S REVENGE

Pelu stopped his march when he saw pillars of smoke rising in the direction of the village they came to rescue. He knew it was too late. Nito's people would not burn down their own village. He called one of the men who had made the earlier trip with Nito to his side and asked him if there were any valleys or large clearings in the route toward the village. It helped that the route they followed was well marked by the several trips in both directions.

"Yes." he said. "Less than a half day's march ahead."

"We go and wait there, then."

They marched double time to the clearing and camped in the woods almost surrounding the open plain. The men deployed in a half circle facing Tong's expected path of return. Pelu assigned four agile climbers to scale the tallest trees in the area and maintain vigilance until relieved every few hours during daylight.

Early afternoon on the second day, the four-treetop watchers descended to warn Pelu of the large contingent of enemy forces they sighted.

The most arduous part of the mission was waiting for the enemy to appear. Pelu instructed his group leaders to wait for his signal before attacking. He wanted to make sure that the bulk of Tong's men were at least halfway into the field before starting his assault. He also ordered a portion of his troops to close the circle from behind once the battle began.

The red man's overconfidence in his power and number of men kept him from sending scouts ahead of his legion. Though tempted, Pelu maintained his patience until he was sure the ambush had the best chance of success. A loud "Kreeeh!" signaled the onslaught. Spears and arrows flew almost in unison, followed by a frightening charge. The once jubilant marauders, though experienced and battle-tested, were shocked into inaction. Their delay, even if only for a few moments, proved fatal. Many died with their spears in carry position and their arcs still over their shoulders.

Mina's selective culling of the painted men came to an abrupt halt when she heard the sounds of battle not far ahead. She assumed that Pelu's expected rescue had now engaged Tong's tribe

Now this was something where the warrior priestess could really display her skills. She abandoned all semblance of stealth and rushed to join the melee.

Mina entered the battle from behind. She shouldered her arc on the run and used her javelin to spear any and all painted warriors in her path. Killing was not totally necessary, a debilitating wound would be enough to incapacitate and remove the injured warrior from further participation. She feared that her father or grandfather may not appreciate or approve of her lust for blood, but the memory of her slain friends and family in the recently decimated village, put aside any thoughts or consideration of mercy.

Pelu had one target, the red-hued Chief Tong. He flew through the throng of enemy combatants, disregarding their presence and the danger they posed. Pelu finally neared the opposing chief and prepared to engage him. Pelu held a short spear in his left hand and a battle-ax in his right. The two war chiefs appraised each other, oblivious to the raging struggle around them. Tong's quick analysis of the engagement around him forced him to make the first move. His best chance was to quickly kill Pelu and make his escape. He would soon discover that killing a highly motivated and skilled opponent was no easy task.

Similarly, Mina also had one primary target herself. She saw Pelu and Tong circling each other as two tigers would while fighting for territory or a mate. Her next action came from the deep recesses of her rage. "Pelu, He is mine. He killed my people and he is mine to destroy."

Pelu was somewhat shocked. He had heard of Mina's exploits but had his doubts of her chance of success in a battle with Tong. Still, something inside him told him he had no choice. He stepped back and told the girl, "He is yours, but I will protect your back from interlopers."

In a flash the words of her late grandfather, Og came back to her. *"Mina, you have proven to be brave as well as skilled, but remember, no matter how good you may believe you are, there is always somebody better. Do not let overconfidence betray you. Know your enemy, end any battle quickly and preferably from a distance."* With those wise words in her mind, Mina did not waste time circling or gesturing. She let her javelin fly and struck Tong on the right thigh. "Ha, yelled Tong, your aim is off. Leg wounds do not kill."

"No, she answered, but they do slow you down."

The fighting in the vicinity slowed and nearly came to a halt as warriors from both sides paused to watch this apparent mismatch. A grown warrior chief confronted by a mere child, and a female, at that.

In one deft move, Mina unshouldered her bow, notched a flet and sent it into the red man's abdomen who fell to his knees in agonizing pain

She then rushed the shocked and critically wounded man, pulled her battle axe and said. "Mine is the last face you will ever see." With that said, she separated Tong's head from his body.

Pelu had been mesmerized during the brief but deadly struggle. Upon returning to reality, He saw that the battle was practically over. Before Tong's head stopped rolling, Mina had dropped her axe, notched a flet and prepared to select targets. Tong's men, after witnessing the impossible, had no interest in facing the little she demon, nor Pelu's army.

Many ran into the woods while others knelt in surrender.

The victorious chief considered inviting the vanquished to join his tribe but chose instead to set them free. He could not take a chance that they would betray him in his own village. Better to let them go and kill them later, if they were foolish enough to challenge him, and Mina again.

After a brief celebration and getting information about survivors from Mina, Pelu found several female hostages taken by Tong and with Mina's help tried to ease their fears and make them comfortable. He had learned much of their language during Nito's visit. The women told him of the raid and destroyed village, but they added that some people had escaped. Pelu was also amazed that Mina was a skilled leader and learned that she was honored as one their tribe's priestesses.

There was no sense in resuming his march to a village full of rotting corpses. Pelu decided to go back home and take the former captives with him. He sent a small party to search for survivors but to return within a moon if none were found.

The march home took longer than usual because his people did not leave their wounded in the field. The surprise attack had worked so well that the Crom's fatalities were few, and the number of wounded was unexpectedly low. They constructed litters to carry those unable to walk. Pelu was surprised but pleased that the women from the pillaged village were no strangers to hard work and took turns pulling litters. Some also displayed skill in caring for wounds. Pelu insisted that Mina walk alongside him on the trek back to his village. He had a lot of questions for the young lady, especially about their spirits and gods. The time she spent with Neru learning his language proved to be worthwhile. Mina also used the opportunity to absorb as much knowledge from the warrior chief in addition to doing her job as Gia's priestess and indoctrinating her host. Og would have been proud.

CHAPTER 31
FAMILY REUNION

The men sent to look for survivors were unfamiliar with the terrain, and the horrid odors from the many dead kept them from getting too close. They circled wide and got some relief when they were upwind from the carnage. They had to be additionally wary in fear that scavenging beasts, attracted by the smell, might prefer a fresh kill. They eventually came across a trail left by numerous people whose tracks suggested a hasty departure. They followed it for the rest of the day but stopped for the night in a quickly erected shelter.

In the morning, the trail was still clear. At midday, they spied some activity at the foot of a small mountain not far ahead.

The people on the mountain were Og's extended family. Tor and his sons were there, along with an assortment of nephews, nieces, and cousins. Nito recognized Pelu's people from a distance and eased the minds of his companions. Nito translated the news delivered by Pelu's warriors: There was no longer a need to worry about the enemy; the red man and his minions were no longer a concern. Pelu's army had met them on the way back after the village was sacked, and they had destroyed most of them. The few remaining would not cause problems for a long time. In the telling, they held back no words of high praise for Mina. Her relentless pursuit, slaying of many assailants and her valiant and quick take down of the attackers' chief were already legendary.

Despite the news that his daughter was well and that she had proven herself a true warrior, Tor was in a somber mood. Aside from having lost his village and many friends, his mother, Su, had not survived the exodus from their home. They buried her in the general area where Og was entombed. His people did not mark graves and simply allowed the remains to return to nature.

Tor conferred with his family to include them in any decision that would affect them all. They agreed to accompany Pelu's search party back to the rescuers' own faraway land. Tor and his brood were not enough to establish an independent village but could set up adequate lodgings near Pelu's large settlement. Perhaps when their numbers increase, they might be able to build a real village of their own.

CHAPTER 32
ASSIMILATION

The journey to seek safety near Pelu's village took longer than expected. The women and children, not inured to extended travel and the extra precautions required outside the confines of a well-stocked village, slowed the procession.

After arriving and resting for a day, Tor, members of his family, Pelu, and Neru explored the area around the large village, looking for an ideal site for Tor's people to settle and call their own, even if temporarily.

They found a spot near hills with caves that were small but adequate for storage, as well as some caves large enough for small family dwellings. Tor preferred caves to huts, and as the spiritual guide, he got first choice. They needed a chief, but Atu, Nito, and Lon declined. They would rather serve as spiritual guides, whether in this nascent village or in Pelu's. Mina laughed when her father looked at her inquisitively. "No father", she said, it is not yet my time. I have some growing to do and a lot to more lessons to learn."

Tor laughed too and said, "It was just an idle thought in the back of my mind. Someday you'll be all three – warrior, priestess, chief. I pity the fools who may try to challenge you."

Tor called Po, and together they took a walk along the river that would serve as one of their future village's boundaries. "Po, you are the bravest and most skilled warrior among us. You should be chief."

"I will accept, but only if it will not affect our friendship and I can continue to depend on your counsel. Also, consider a role for your daughter, Mina. She has more than exceeded our expectations."

"You have my promise on your requests. However, I fear that my little girl will make plans of her own and will forge a future of her choosing. As for us, we make a good team. You also need a mate. You will not need to hunt anymore, and it is time to start your own family."

"Being chief has its benefits, I see, and it's easy for now because there are so few of us."

"You need to find a mate as soon as possible and start making more of us."

Po smiled and said, "Did you notice that two of the women Pelu rescued from Tong are already pregnant?"

"Yes. That means at least two more members for you to lead."

CHAPTER 33
SPREADING THE WORD OF OG

Several seasons later, Tor and Po sent expeditions to their former lands. They found only whitened bones in their former home but no trace of people from other villages except vague signs of old battles. It appeared as if things had not gone well for them. If any were still alive, they were scattered across the land.

The years passed. Po's tribe increased in numbers as interbreeding between both tribes became commonplace. Ease of communication improved as each group adopted words from each other's lexicons. The improvement in exchange of ideas helped Tor and his family to expand their quest to spread the word of Og. The interchange of knowledge and skills was mutual. Tor's people learned more about fishing, crop growing, building techniques while Pelu's tribe learned how to turn birch tree bark into a glue more effective in assembling weapons. The most important development for Tor was the acceptance of his teachings. He maintained the family tradition, with few exceptions, of selecting only offspring of his progeny to become priests and priestesses and speak for their pantheon of gods.

Tor aged well. Likely because of the inherited genetic makeup from Og, the years were kind to him. His sons were now grown and experienced spiritual leaders for the Crom and their own growing collection of huts and expanding population. Some formed groups that established other villages. Each village was a distinct municipality with its own chief. The one commonality that remained practically intact was the spiritual teachings inspired by Og and refined by Tor and his children.. It continued to flourish under the generations that followed. Tor had begun the indoctrination of Nito's and Fela's children. They and theirs would someday spread the word among other Crom villages. His daughter Lia carried on the tradition with her own, and Neru had been converted long ago.

During the exodus and later, as the tribe resettled around Pelu's compound, Mina remembered her actions during the battle back in her homeland. She appreciated greatly Pelu's attempt to rescue her village and the battle with the painted men. She was most fond of her own duel with the red hued Tong. She was elated that she had been the one to confront him and exact revenge for her devastated native village.

The young woman had not put aside her dreams of becoming a tribal chief but added to her plans by insisting that her brother Atu fine-tune her instruction on all spiritual matters. Mina also requested that Po continue as her mentor to hone her skills in the art of war. She also studied and absorbed his leadership techniques as chief. She wanted to be a village chief as well as its warlord and priestess.

As she grew stronger, she finally achieved her goal of wielding the battle-axe better than any man. It was her weapon of choice in close quarter combat. Her skill at hitting a target at a distance with a hurled axe became the envy of all.

She had postponed her goal of hunting and dominating a giant cave bear by herself until reaching true womanhood. It would have been folly to attempt the feat with the build and muscles of a child.

When it came to be, it turned out to be an unfair match. She came across a big bear slurping honey from a damaged beehive. The bear turned nonchalantly toward her. It must have been in a slight stupor from gorging itself with honey as it sauntered lazily toward Mina. It was a huge beast and Mina could not risk a sudden change in the animal's intent or disposition. Besides, her nascent village could use more meat. She pulled her battle axe and hurled it with all her considerable strength. It struck the beast between the eyes but with the blunt end. The blow did not kill it but knocked it into a dazed state. The first flet hit below the throat, it rose on its hind leges but could only produce a gurgled roar. Mina produced her short spear and let it fly. It entered the chest and as the bear came down on all four, the ground pushed the spear deeper into its heart. As had become her custom, the huntress gave way to the priestess within her who thanked Gia for providing sustenance for her tribe.

Mina gathered her flock and went back some of them to collect the bounty. Nito happened to be visiting and told her that their father would be very proud, as well as the remnants of their old tribe,

In time, Mina found a mate among the Crom and with a few others of their respective clans established her own small village where she fulfilled her dreams and emerged as one of the first female chieftains and priestess. The one thing that surprised her during her spiritual indoctrination were the intricacies of the elaborate fantasy that Grandfather Og had weaved out of pure imagination and then imbedded in the minds of an entire population. She had always had her suspicions and doubts but it was not her place to question her parents or grandfather. Besides, up until the time of the invasion, all had been well. Now when it was her turn to continue the family legacy, she was not about to disavow a program that had worked so well for so much of her life. Mina was determined to continue her father's and grandfather's ways while adding a few touches of her own.

Under her leadership as chief and high priestess she eventually founded elaborate villages in her own territories. She emphasized that women play major roles as priestesses and warriors while also respecting the important roles that men played. Her daughters were indoctrinated as priestesses to speak for the growing population of goddesses under Mother Gia. Atha, the spirit protector of female warriors received the most attention and offerings from Mina's growing army of fearless fighters.

Mina lived a long and fruitful life. She added to her religious observances the building of temples to honor the many spirits whom she credited with her people's accomplishments and rich, adventurous lives. Her descendants would continue to prosper for many years, gaining fame for unmatched exploits in battle and innovations. Her people would one day domesticate the horse and develop the strategy of mounted warfare to protect their lands and cities.

Tor in his stead believed he had followed through in his promise to Og to keep his teachings alive. He was also becoming restless. His mate had died moons ago, and he had been loath to choose another. Yet, he needed an adventure. Crom travelers told stories of vast tracts of land to the east and villages that were ignorant of the existence of spirits. Even though he was anxious for change, Tor preferred to plan instead of rushing into the unfamiliar.

While he pondered his future, Tor found Mila, an interested female in the Crom village. She was the young widow of a warrior who'd lost his life while defending Tor's previous home. With a young mate, now he needed other companion adventurers. His grandson from Atu was old enough and was eager to travel with his grandfather. Nito also had a son anxious to explore. Two young Crom friends of Tor's grandsons volunteered without needing persuasion. The expedition now consisted of Tor; his mate, Mila; his grandsons Aru and Sito; and their two friends Loro and Bolu. The four young men managed to convince their female friends to join them in their quest. As the travelling band prepared to leave, several other young men and women were captivated by their enthusiasm, embraced the spirit of adventure and joined the quest to no specific destination. Tor was elated; the more their number, the greater chance of survival and success.

They bid their families and friends farewell and began a journey destined to continue for years for themselves and many more years for a long line of descendants. Eventually, they traversed what is now the Middle East and Asia. They came across other tribes on the journey that had no preset destination. They recruited new companions along the way. As their numbers increased, some of the travelling band found favorable sites and chose to stay behind to establish their own new lives. Others found favor with existing clans along the way, joined them, and eventually became assimilated into those groups. Among those who broke off from the wandering explorers were spiritual leaders ordained by Tor or his progeny. Their inherent sense of duty was to pass on the old teachings begun by their long-dead spiritual patriarch. Tor and his band of wanderers headed mostly east. His warrior daughter Mina and her group veered southeast.

Tor lived even longer than his father Og had. He fathered many children during his odyssey, and each one learned and practiced the words of Og. Tor himself did not make it to the new continent, and his companions did not realize that they had crossed into a world where they were the first humans. Tor's physical body remained behind in an unmarked grave, but his teachings, rituals, beliefs, and tales of his family's legendary lives were carried forward in the minds and spirits of his progeny.

Descendants of the original migrant explorers that took an easterly route, gradually numbered in the hundreds and crossed the Bering Strait. They turned south to the lands now called North and South America. During the ensuing millennia, they spread throughout every habitable area of their new world. They split into separate groups, which eventually formed indigenous tribes from the Pacific Ocean and across the plains to the Atlantic Ocean. Some ventured farther south and became Aztec, Mayan, Toltecs, Incas, and many other civilizations in which religious beliefs and practices played a very important and, in some cases, dominant part and in others, a corrupted version which practiced human sacrifice. Others took to the seas hop-scotching small islands and populating the larger islands of the Caribbean as Arawak, Caribs and Taino. A few groups, by chance or by design, came across distant islands and also flourished.

The lineage of the first priest, who remained in the old world and survived the harsh conditions of that era, eventually prospered and gave rise to nations all over Europe, Middle East, and Asia. They also carried on the spiritual teachings of their ancestors, although in many cases, the teachings were altered with the passage of time, and corrupted by greed or lust for power.

The legend of Og faded into obscurity, but his original creation of persuasive idolization spread throughout the old and new world and carried on into the future of now.

The End

EPILOGUE

As humans developed social and family groups for mutual protection, procreation, and survival of the species, a need for leaders arose. A patriarch or matriarch for smaller family units, and a chief or leader for larger groups, became the norm. Leadership positions usually passed on via heredity, and sometimes by way of combat. Priests, shamans, or other spiritual guides may have maintained the same hierarchy by teaching their sons and daughters to carry on the family tradition. Throughout history, kings, queens, pharaohs, and even popes made every effort to keep family members in power. The Medici family held papal power from 1513 to 1605, plus royal seats of power during the sixteenth to the eighteenth century in France and in sections of Italy (Medici Family 2017). Likewise, the Borgia clan ruled church and states during the fifteenth century and into the sixteenth century (Lagasse 2017). It is not a stretch to imagine that earlier humans employed the same hereditary methods to keep political or religious influence within family circles.

Although the village of Og grew and flourished for many years, the utopian future he visualized for his people was not to be. The creeping ice age made its way down from the north. From the east came a different form of man: taller, slimmer, more agile, better armed, and more evolved for survival.

Og's descendants found that no amount of prayer or bloody sacrifice could stop the deadly, bitter cold and encroaching ice. In time, nature and the newcomers edged them out of their accustomed habitat. There was comingling with the interlopers, and although they added to the new people's genetic pool, the species as a whole ceased to exist.

Og's people became mere DNA fragments in the future of humanity, but his nascent religious ideas, in a myriad of forms and incarnations, were never abandoned and became the strongest persuasive force ever created.

HISTORICAL NOTES

The following information includes findings, theories or conclusions published before and after, the writing of this novel. Ongoing research disputes or alters previous findings and presents revised data. Other than cave art there is no written evidence of what occurred so many millennia ago. Archeology is subject to interpretation, dating methods are not 100% accurate and even DNA evidence is questioned by some. Definitive proof or evidence may never be found. We can however come to accept (many) conclusions with some degree of confidence that the findings are reasonably accurate.

From about 1848 on, hundreds of Neanderthal bones were discovered from Gibraltar and across Europe to the Himalayas. Fossils found in Germany's Neander Valley led to the name Neanderthal. It is believed that modern man's cousins lived in what is now Europe and Asia from about 200,000 years ago until about 10,000 years BC.

Early archeologists and anthropologists assembled Neanderthal bones incorrectly, depicting Neanderthals as having bowed legs and hunched backs. The error in the reconstruction of the skeleton led researchers to believe that they walked with an apelike shuffle. Later corrections show them standing upright like modern man. Improved archeological methods, modern scanning, and x-ray equipment helped researchers discount many other erroneous conclusions and assumptions. The most important discoveries came about after sufficient DNA samples became available for scientists to decode.

A complete Neanderthal skeleton has yet to be found. In order to create a complete model, Gary Sawyer, an expert in skeletal reconstruction from the American Museum of Natural History in New York, used the fictional Dr. Frankenstein's method of assembling one using parts from various specimens. The result was a five foot four, powerfully built male. It had a barrel chest and a substantial abdominal area. Neanderthals were not slim waisted. The short, compact body was suited for survival in very cold climates. Researchers estimate that Neanderthals may have been as much as six times stronger than modern humans. Despite their adaptability and apparent robust physique, their life spans were short compared to today's population: the average life span was about thirty years. The oldest specimen found appears to have reached forty-five years of age; he was riddled with arthritis and had few teeth left. The harsh environment, dangerous lifestyle, predators, and disease also did not contribute to longevity.

After the assembling of a full-size skeleton, it was the job of Ralph Holloway, Columbia University, and an expert in the anatomy of ancient brains to determine their intellectual capability. The size of the skull suggests the Neanderthal brain was about 20 percent larger than those of modern humans. A cast formed from the imprint of the interior of the skull determined that the symmetry of the subject brain was the same as modern man. The frontal and prefrontal lobes were also the same. The conclusion was that cognitive function had to be similar to current humans.

The next step was to determine linguistic abilities. Professor Bob Franciscus, an anthropologist and expert in noses and throats, examined a Neanderthal hyoid bone, which is essential for speech. He had to artificially reconstruct the soft tissue that surrounds the bone. The resulting vocal tract was shorter and wider than present humans but was anatomically similar enough to enable speech. Another expert, voice specialist Patsy Rodenburg, determined the possible pitch of a Neanderthal's voice after considering known factors of shape of the vocal tract, the deep rib cage, the powerful chest, and even the weight of the skull.

These studies negate the previous beliefs that Neanderthals were apelike, brutish beasts of limited intellect, speechless, and generally inferior to later humans.

"The public image of Neanderthals as low-browed, hulking brutes is due for a makeover. Humans sometimes like to think of themselves as quite distinct from their extinct cousins, but the evidence from more and more fossil sites suggests that Homo neanderthalensis and Homo sapiens shared many personal qualities" (Ackerman 2017).

In the last several years since the sequencing of the Neanderthal genetic code, old assumptions or conclusions are undergoing radical changes. It is clear that Cro-Magnon and Neanderthals coexisted and even interbred for several thousand years. Some early sources estimated the period of interactivity between the two lasted from 5,400 to up to 10,000 years, but a more recent study (UPR) revised previous estimates that suggest the two species comingled for up to 30,000 years. Neanderthals did not go extinct due to a cataclysmic event. Their numbers may have diminished due to a sudden change in weather prior to the arrival of the new men. Sufficient numbers remained to interact and breed with the newcomers. Finally, they were rather slowly assimilated into the growing population of modern man. Genetic studies and sampling estimate that present day Europeans and Asians carry 1 percent to as high as 4 percent of Neanderthal DNA. Early migration patterns indicate the flow of explorers or nomads went north out of Africa and not in reverse, and so Neanderthal DNA is rare or nonexistent in people of African descent.

It appears that modern man can be thankful to Neanderthals for passing on a sequence of genes, Human Leukocyte Antigens (HLA), that regulate the immune system and help resist disease. They also gave modern humans susceptibility to allergies, so the exchange was not always positive (Max Planck Inst 2010).

The following citations from varied research projects are further indications that there were definite interactions between Neanderthals and other hominids that were anatomically and intellectually close to the modern versions of humans. The term *Cro-Magnon,* referring to the people that coexisted with Neanderthals, is no longer generally used. The designations now preferred are anatomically modern humans (AMH) or early modern humans (EMH). The larger EMH population eventually absorbed or assimilated the fewer number of Neanderthals.

When modern humans met Neanderthals in Europe and the two species began interbreeding many thousands of years ago, the exchange left humans with gene variations that have increased the ability of those who carry them to ward off infection. (Cell Press 2016)

We found that interbreeding with archaic humans—the Neanderthals and Denisovans—has influenced the genetic diversity in present-day genomes at three innate immunity genes belonging to the human Toll-like-receptor family. (Kelso 2016)

These TLR genes are expressed on the cell surface, where they detect and respond to components of bacteria, fungi, and parasites. (Dannemann 2016)

Other recent archeological findings suggest that Neanderthals understood art and symbolism, and they practiced rituals, further demonstrating spiritual awareness. They may have used feathers and shells as ornaments, and they applied tattoos and body paint. The researchers determined that crossbreeding may have led to the acquisition of other significant traits and features such as sleep patterns, skin pigmentation, hair color, and other characteristics.

Further research at the Max Planck Institute continued to determine the extent of "influence Neanderthal DNA might be having on ordinary variation in people today" (Kelso 2017).

When starting this book, I gave the Neanderthal characters monosyllabic names under the impression that their language was primitive and likely consisted of little more than grunts and signs. That assumption appears to be false. In later research, I discovered that Neanderthal genetic mapping determined that the DNA sequence in the area of language was identical to modern humans. Their language may have been as complex as modern speech. With apologies to ancestors who contributed a small percentage to my own DNA, I did not rewrite to give them more complex names.

Although sophisticated metallurgy did not become an art until about 5000 BC, naturally occurring metals were known to early humans, and some found uses for them as decorations, such as gold and silver. They used harder metals as weapons.

Early hominids probably used rocks as their first weapons and progressed to clubs or other similar handheld items. Archeological evidence indicates that the spear came into use 500,000–780,000 years ago. The bow and arrow appeared about 64,000 years ago, and the atlatl developed sometime in between the two weapon systems (Rhodes 2013).

Three significant weapon systems appear during the Stone Age, which, in concert with other basic survival strategies, helped early humans to survive and then thrive under often extremely adverse conditions. (Rhodes 2013)

Neanderthals developed a unique dry distillation method to produce heated birch glue used to attach spear points to their shafts. The ancient process has been duplicated under modern laboratory conditions, but only in small amounts.

Abilities to precisely control fire temperatures and to manipulate adhesive properties are believed to require advanced mental traits ... Neanderthals must have been able to recognize certain material properties, such as adhesive tack and viscosity. (Kozowyk et al. 2017)

There is historical evidence to suggest that the character Mina could have assumed spiritual or general leadership of a tribe or area.

Archeological studies suggest that some late Paleolithic and early Neolithic societies in Europe may have been matriarchies, matrilineal or matrifocal. Most researchers avoid the term matriarchy because it denotes full autocratic rule by women instead of matrifocal, which indicates women, usually mothers, holding a central position but not a dominating one. Studies show that goddesses and priestesses were also prominent.

"...we do not find in Old Europe nor in all the Old World, a system of autocratic rule by women with an equivalent suppression of men. Rather we find a structure in which the sexes are more or less on equal footing, a society that could be termed a *gylany*

[in which] the sexes are 'linked' rather than hierarchically 'ranked.' I use the term matristic to avoid the term matriarchy, with the understanding that it incorporates matriliny." (Gimbutas 1991:324)

According to some studies, the mythological Amazons did not originate in South America but instead in an area of Eurasia known as Scythia. The society is estimated to have existed from 1100 BC to about 200 AD.

Scythian women may have been the original Amazons. The name has become synonymous with female warriors. The Amazons are believed to have established cities and built temples in Smyrna, Sinope, Gryne, Ephesus and others in the area now known as the Ukraine, Russsia and Crimea. They are also credited with inventing the cavalry. Simon, W. Foreman, A. (n.d.)

ABOUT THE AUTHOR

Mr. Jaime Reyes has enjoyed many career changes. He was born in Arecibo, Puerto Rico, several decades ago. His family moved to the US mainland when he was nearly eight years old. He spoke no English but in a matter of months was fluent enough to become a straight A student. It helped that he learned to read Spanish at age three and continued to feed his voracious appetite for words in the new language.

After graduating from Thomas A. Edison High School, he was drafted into the US Army and served honorably in Vietnam as a military intelligence agent and analyst. After completing military service, he started his own business, which he managed successfully for seven years.

He sold the business and pursued the career of his dreams in law enforcement. He worked with the Philadelphia Police Department for five years and then the Philadelphia Office of the Sheriff as a deputy sheriff. He served for twenty-five years, the last ten years as a supervisor. During off hours, he wrote articles as a hobby in English and Spanish, including opinion pieces, guest columns, and public service articles in various newspapers and online publications.

After retiring from law enforcement, he wanted to establish credentials to continue a writing career, and so he earned a bachelor's in communication and journalism at an age when most people are enjoying a leisurely retirement. As a result of having read hundreds of books, he used CLEP (College Level Examination Program) and other similar programs to test out of elective courses and earn his degree in just two years.

He continued writing articles and short stories. The short story version of *In the Beginning* received good reviews, and he decided to convert it to a novel. An incentive for the short story and the book came from a genealogical study that determined that his varied ancestral lineage includes three percent Neanderthal DNA.

In the Beginning is his first published book.

SOURCES

Ackerman, S. J. 2017. "Neanderthals Revisited." *American Scientist* 105, no. 1 (Jan/Feb): 6–7.

Borgia. 2017. In P. Lagasse, Columbia University, *The Columbia Encyclopedia,* 7th edition, New York: Columbia University Press. Retrieved from http://search.credoreference.com.contentproxy. phoenix.edu/content/entry/columency/borgia/0.

Cell Press. 2017. "More Traits Associated with Your Neanderthal DNA." *Science Daily.* October 5. www.sciencedaily.com/ releases/2017/10/171005121106.htm.

Cell Press. 2016. "Neanderthal Genes Gave Modern Humans an Immunity Boost, Allergies." *Science Daily,* January 7. www. sciencedaily.com/releases/2016/01/160107140408.htm.

Dannemann, Michael, Aida M. Andrés, and Janet Kelso. 2016. **"Introgression of Neandertal- and Denisovan-like Haplotypes Contributes to Adaptive Variation in Human Toll-like Receptors."** *American Journal of Human Genetics* 98, no. 1:22. DOI: 10.1016/j.ajhg.2015.11.015.

Dannemann, Michael, and Janet Kelso. 2017. **"The Contribution of Neandertals to Phenotypic Variation in Modern Humans."** *American Journal of Human Genetics.* 10.1016/j.ajhg.2017.09.010.

Deschamps, Matthieu, Guillaume Laval, Maud Fagny, Yuval Itan, Laurent Abel, Jean-Laurent Casanova, Etienne Patin, and Lluis Quintana-Murci. 2016. **"Genomic Signatures of Selective Pressures and Introgression from Archaic Hominins at Human Innate Immunity Genes."** *American Journal of Human Genetics* 98, no. 1:5. DOI: 10.1016/j.ajhg.2015.11.014.

Kozowyk, P. R. B., M. Soressi; D. Pomstra, and G. H. Langejans. 2017. "Experimental Methods for the Palaeolithic Dry Distillation of Birch Bark: Implications for the Origin and Development of Neanderthal Adhesive Technology." *Scientific Reports* 7 (Aug): 1–9.

"Medici Family." 2017. In *Encyclopædia Britannica*. Retrieved from http://academic.eb.com.contentproxy.phoenix.edu/levels/collegiate/article/Medici-family/51736.

Rhodes, H. 2013. "Taking Ownership of Distance in the Stone Age with Spear, Atlatl, and Archery: Prehistoric Weapon Systems and the Domination of Distance." *Comparative Civilizations Review*, no. 69 (Fall): 45–53.

Universitat Bonn. 2013. "Immune Gene in Humans Inherited from Neanderthals, Study Suggests." *Science Daily*, November 22. www.sciencedaily.com/releases/2013/131122084405.htm.

University of Oxford. 2014. "Neanderthals 'Overlapped' with Modern Humans for up to 5400 Years." *Science Daily*, August 21. www.sciencedaily.com/releases/2014/08/140821123757.htm.

John Marler n.d. The Iconography and Social Structure of Old Europe: The Archeological Research of Marija Gimbutas. Retrieved from:

http://www.second-congress-matriarchal-studies.com/marler.html

Tacitus, C. 98 AD. Germania. Retrieved from https://en.wikipedia.org/wiki/Matriarchy

Foreman, Amanda. "The Amazon Women: Is There Any Truth Behind the Myth?". *Smithsonian.com. Smithsonian Institution.* Retrieved from https://en.wikipedia.org/wiki/Matriarchy

Simon, Worrall. "Amazon Warriors Did Indeed Fight and Die Like Men". *National Geographic.* Retrieved from https://en.wikipedia.org/wiki/Matriarchy & https://en.wikipedia.org/wiki/Scythians

FYI

The following video links provide more information on
Neanderthals and early modern humans.

https://www.youtube.com/watch?v=RrfTp0eUuB4
https://www.youtube.com/watch?v=6hIyD1QlX9k
https://www.youtube.com/watch?v=sSANyOtEalg
https://www.youtube.com/watch?v=5sM7Tr8qlvU
https://www.youtube.com/watch?v=dWKCdChaLn0

CONTACT THE AUTHOR

Twitter: @Rey3J
Facebook: James Rey
Website: www.jreyesauthor.com
Word Press: http://jrey3.com
Email: j_rey3@yahoo.com

Coming soon:

First Night by Jaime Reyes

Historical Fiction Vietnam novel. More historical with slight touches of fiction to protect the innocent, the culpable and to avoid embarrassment or painful memories to any who may recognize an actual similar event.

Javier had just laid his head down on his cot. The first shot startled him. *Oh hell, I'm going to die on my first night,* he thought as he reached under his pillow for his issued weapon, a five shot snub nose revolver. His second thought centered around his meager defensive weapon – the enemy was armed with AK-47s at least. What good is this piece of crap.

He ran to the Quonset hut door just in time to see his recently acquired friend, Sgt Miranda run towards a prone body and empty his M-16 into the downed soldier. Then more shock as the compound guard fired one shot at the sergeant, hitting him in the thigh.

"What the hell, we're shooting each other!" Javier said to no one in particular.

Thank You
JR